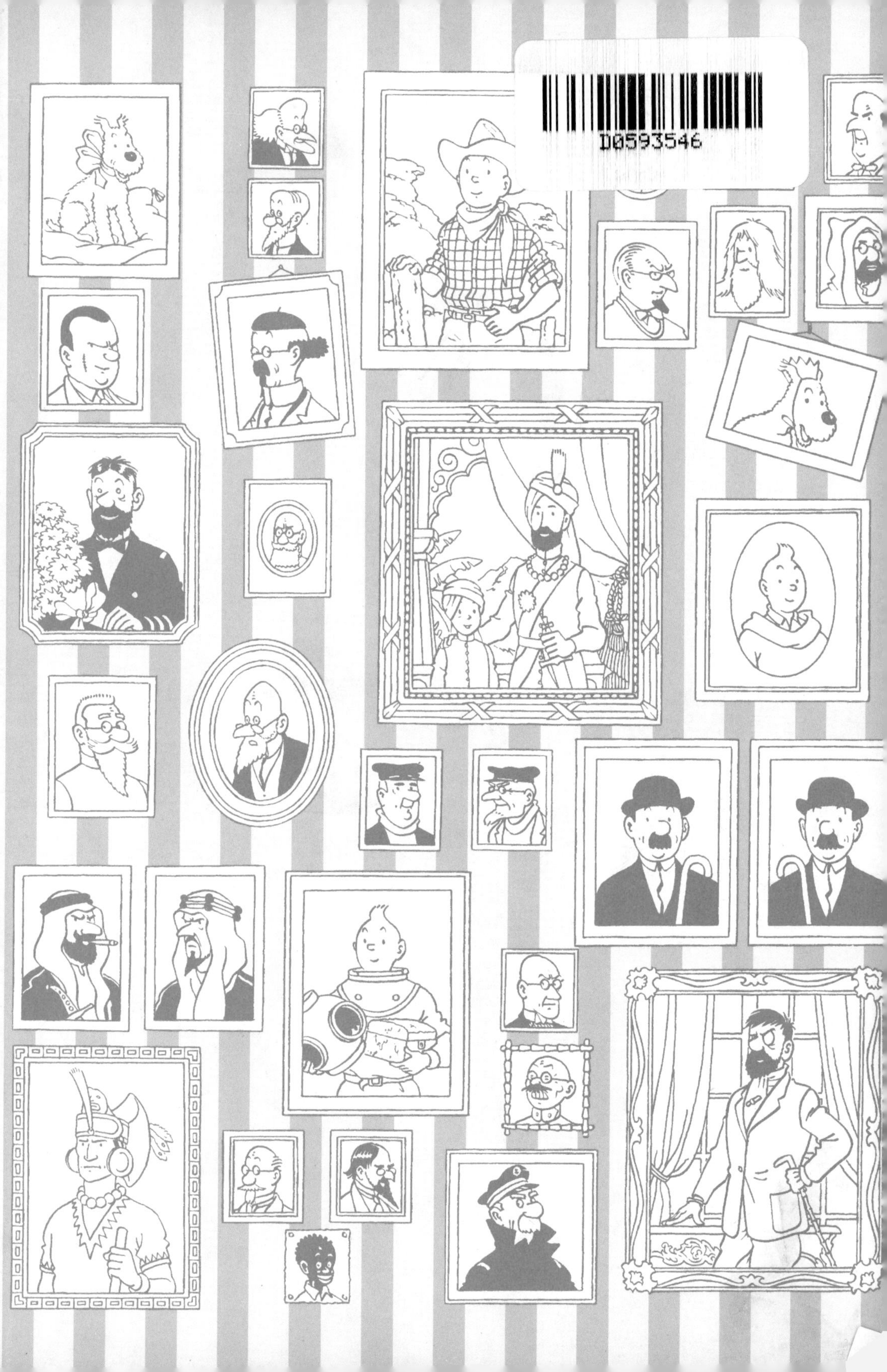

HERGÉ

THE ADVENTURES OF TINTIN

THE BROKEN EAR

LITTLE, BROWN AND COMPANY
BOSTON/NEW YORK/TORONTO/LONDON

Translated by Leslie Lonsdale-Cooper
and Michael Turner

Also available from Little, Brown
in the TINTIN THREE-IN-ONE series:

Volume 1: TINTIN IN AMERICA
CIGARS OF THE PHARAOH
THE BLUE LOTUS

Volume 3: THE CRAB WITH THE GOLDEN CLAWS
THE SHOOTING STAR
THE SECRET OF THE UNICORN

Afrikaans :		HUMAN & ROUSSEAU, Cape Town.
Arabic :		DAR AL-MAAREF, Cairo.
Basque :		MENSAJERO, Bilbao.
Brazilian :		DISTRIBUIDORA RECORD, Rio de Janeiro.
Breton :		CASTERMAN, Paris.
Catalan :		JUVENTUD, Barcelona.
Chinese :		EPOCH, Taipei.
Danish :		CARLSEN IF, Copenhagen.
Dutch :		CASTERMAN, Dronten.
English :	U.K. :	METHUEN CHILDREN'S BOOKS, London.
	Australia :	REED PUBLISHING AUSTRALIA, Melbourne.
	Canada :	REED PUBLISHING CANADA, Toronto.
	New Zealand :	REED PUBLISHING NEW ZEALAND, Auckland.
	Republic of South Africa :	STRUIK BOOK DISTRIBUTORS, Johannesburg.
	Singapore :	REED PUBLISHING ASIA, Singapore.
	Spain :	EDICIONES DEL PRADO, Madrid.
	Portugal :	EDICIONES DEL PRADO, Madrid.
	U.S.A.	LITTLE BROWN, Boston.
Esperanto :		CASTERMAN, Paris.
Finnish :		OTAVA, Helsinki.
French :		CASTERMAN, Paris-Tournai.
	Spain :	EDICIONES DEL PRADO, Madrid.
	Portugal :	EDICIONES DEL PRADO, Madrid.
Galician :		JUVENTUD, Barcelona.
German :		CARLSEN, Reinbek-Hamburg.
Greek :		ANGLO-HELLENIC, Athens.
Icelandic :		FJÖLVI, Reykjavik.
Indonesian :		INDIRA, Jakarta.
Iranian :		MODERN PRINTING HOUSE, Teheran.
Italian :		GANDUS, Genoa.
Japanese :		FUKUINKAN SHOTEN, Tokyo.
Korean :		UNIVERSAL PUBLICATIONS, Seoul.
Malay :		SHARIKAT UNITED, Pulau Pinang.
Norwegian :		SEMIC, Oslo.
Picard :		CASTERMAN, Paris.
Portuguese :		CENTRO DO LIVRO BRASILEIRO, Lisboa.
Provençal :		CASTERMAN, Paris.
Spanish :		JUVENTUD, Barcelona.
	Argentina :	JUVENTUD ARGENTINA, Buenos Aires.
	Mexico :	MARIN, Mexico.
	Peru :	DISTR. DE LIBROS DEL PACIFICO, Lima.
Serbo-Croatian :		DECJE NOVINE, Gornji Milanovac.
Swedish :		CARLSEN IF, Stockholm.
Welsh :		GWASG Y DREF WEN, Cardiff.

Tintin and the Broken Ear
Artwork copyright © 1945 by Editions Casterman, Tournai
Translation text copyright © 1975 by Methuen Children's Books
American edition copyright © 1978 by Little, Brown and Company

This edition first published in Great Britain in 1990 by
Methuen Children's Books.

Library of Congress Catalog Card Number: 93-80119
ISBN: 0-316-35942-4
10 9 8 7 6 5 4 3 2 1
Printed in Belgium by Casterman S.A.

PAINTED POSTS DAHOMEY

BAPENDE MASK

HEAD OF CARVED WOOD PACHACAMAC

No. 3542
ARUMBAYA FETISH
The Arumbaya tribe live along the banks of the River Coliflor in the Republic of San Theodoros, South America

Closing time!

Goodness! It's five o'clock already...

RRRRING

Come on, lazy-bones! Time to get up!

Toreador, on guard now! Toreador! Torea dor! Toreador!

Toreador... tra la la la la... Toreador... Fond eyes gaze and adore...

PLURIARC BURMA

Knees bent, arms full stretch! Ready...Up... and down... and up... and down...

Now for a bath; that's the way to wake up in the morning.

Here is the eight o'clock news...

Details are just coming in of a robbery at the Museum of Ethnography. A rare fetish - a sacred tribal object - disappeared during the night...

The loss was discovered this morning by a museum attendant. It is believed the thief must have hidden in the gallery overnight and slipped out when the staff arrived for work. No evidence of a break-in has been found...

Come on Snowy! To the Museum of Ethnography!

The Director? I'm afraid he's engaged: the police are here...

Now, to recapitulate...You say the attendant locked the doors last night at 1712 hours; he noticed nothing unusual. He came on duty this morning at seven. At 0714 he observed that exhibit No. 3542 was missing and immediately raised the alarm. Right?...Now this attendant: is he reliable?

Absolutely! Above suspicion! He's been with us for over twelve years and never given the least cause for complaint.

Besides, the fetish has no intrinsic value. In my judgement, it would only be of interest to a collector...

Great snakes! The Thompsons!

Why, it's our friend Tintin!

Have you any leads?

Well, the Arumbaya fetish has no in...er... no instinctive value...The solution is quite simple: it was removed by a collector.

To be precise: it was collect—ed by a re—mover.

Some hours later...

This is the book. I'm sure it has something about the Arumbayas.

A.J. WALKER

TRAVELS IN THE AMERICAS

LONDON 1875

Aha! This is interesting...Listen, Snowy. "Today we met our first Arumbayas. Long, black, oily hair framed their coffee-coloured faces. They were armed with long blowpipes which they employ to shoot darts poisoned with curare..." You hear that, Snowy?

...We decided to stay there. The sun generosity and gave us a plentiful

ARUMBAYA
armed with a blow-pipe

...Curare!...the terrible vegetable poison which paralyses one's breathing!...Oh! "Arumbaya fetish"...But...but...it's the very one that's been stolen!

...I so say; Mot I therefore made an accurate sketch they urged me to go

ARUMBAYA
FETISH
we were very well
treated. Later we

Odd coincidence, don't you think, Snowy?... Snowy isn't interested... he's gone to sleep ...I think I'll follow suit.

The next morning...

Help! It's bewitched!

Hello!...Hello?... Hello!?... Is that you, sir?

Yes, who is that? ...Oh, it's you, Fred...What? The fetish?...My goodness me! I'll come at once...

(4)

Extraordinary! There was the fetish this morning, back in its usual place, with this letter propped up beside it... What do you think?
Hmmm!
Hmm?
In my opinion, gentlemen, the fetish is bewitched!
Dear Director,
I bet a friend I could pinch something from your museum.
I won my bet, so here's your fetish back.
Please forgive my foolishness, and any trouble I have caused.
Sincerely,
X
!
No. 3542
ARUMBAYA FETISH
The Arumbaya tribe live along the banks of the River Coliflor in the Republic of San Theodoros,
My mind is made up: this letter is anonymous. Nobody knows who wrote it!
To be precise: I agree. An anonymous letter nobody wrote!
According to the police the case is closed... But that isn't my view...
Why doesn't he give up?
I do beg your pardon, sir!
Wake up, Tintin! Look where you're going!
So, am I the only one to know the fetish they put back is a fake?
Here's the proof. Walker, the explorer, says he made an "accurate sketch". And according to the drawing...
... the right ear of the fetish is slightly damaged: there's a little bit missing.
ARUMBAYA FETISH
But on the reinstated fetish the right ear is intact. So it must be a copy... Now, who would be interested in acquiring the real one? A collector? Quite possibly... Anyway, let's see what the press has to say about it.
Oh dear, here we go again... Sherlock Holmes on the trail!
!....
FATAL OVERSIGHT
A strong smell of gas alerted residents this morning at 21 London Road. They sent for the police who effected an entry to the room occupied by artist Jacob Balthazar. Officers discovered the sculptor lying on his bed; he was found to be dead. It appears that the victim had forgotten to turn off the tap on his gas-ring. By some chance his parrot survived the fumes.
Mr. Balthazar's work attracted the attention of art-critics, who particularly praised his series of wooden statuettes, his special technique being strongly reminiscent of primitive sculpture.
Going round and round like that, he makes me giddy!

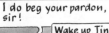

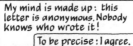

Half an hour later...

Excuse me...Is this the house where Mr. Balthazar lived?

Yes, this is it. Ooh, sir, what a tragedy!...Such a polite gentleman!...And all that learning!...Maybe he wasn't all that regular with the rent, but he always paid it in the end. And such a way with animals! A parrot and three white mice, that's what he had...

I...

I'm minding the parrot for the time being. But I can't keep it. So if you know of anyone...

Of course...I was wondering if I might look at Mr. Balthazar's room?

I'll take you up. Such a character he was...sniff...I can still see him...his ever-lasting black velvet suit, and that big hat...And all that smoking! A pipe in his mouth all day long, he had. But he never touched the drink...

Oh?

Here is his room...

This is where we found him ...sniff...They had to send for a locksmith...the door was locked from the inside...The gas was whistling out of the ring.

A little scrap of grey flannel...

And so clever he was...Just look at those flowers: you can almost smell them...

You knew Mr. Balthazar well?

Er...that's to say...not intimately...

If by any chance you found a parrot-lover...It's such a friendly bird!

Naturally, I'll remember you. Good-bye and thanks.

An accident?...Funny sort of accident, I'd say...

A very funny accident!...The gas was whistling out of the ring. So, if the tap was on when Balthazar went to bed he'd have heard it. Unless he was drunk; but he never touched drink. Therefore someone turned the tap on after the sculptor was dead, since the gas wasn't strong enough to kill the parrot. And that someone was wearing something made of grey flannel and smoking a cigarette...

...witness the piece of cloth and the cigarette end, which couldn't have belonged to the victim: he only smoked a pipe, and he wore a velvet suit. So Mr. Balthazar was murdered. He was murdered because he'd probably made a replica of the Arumbaya fetish for someone. And someone didn't want him to talk... Someone?... Someone? ... Who can that 'someone' be?...How can I find out?

Great snakes!... Why not ?!

Excuse me, but I've been thinking. I'll buy Mr. Balthazar's parrot.

The parrot? Ooooh, sir!

If you'd only been two minutes sooner! I just sold it. The gentleman who bought it was here a moment ago; you must have passed him.

Just my luck!

Look, there he goes! You see the gentleman with a parcel under his arm? That's him.

Let's hope he'll agree to resell it to me.

Grrreat greedy-guts!

Hey, you!...D'you always behave like that! Let me tell you, I'm not used to being insulted!

Perdone, Señor.

Very well! But another time you'll be in trouble!

But...I assure the señor...

GRRREAT GREEDY-GUTS!

Oh, help! It's a regular punch-up...Ooh! The parrot! The parrot!!

The parrot!!!

GRRREAT GREEDY-GUTS!

Estúpido! Imbécil! Great greedy-guts! Look what you do: my beautiful parrot ees escapado! Ees perdido!

The only witness to Balthazar's death, the only one who could have talked, and there he goes.

The parrot ees give me by my grandfather. Ay, qué desastre...All same, muchas gracias for try to catch heem.

That's quite all right.

"Give to me by my grandfather." Why tell a lie? I wonder, could he be interested in the parrot for the same reason as me?

7

Meanwhile...

It's raining, Professor. Don't forget your umbrella ...and remember your glasses.

Don't worry, Ernestine. My glasses are in the pocket of my jacket...and I'll take my umbrella.

PWARK

PWARK PWARK

?

What a curious-looking creature!

I must take a closer look...Now, where have my glasses gone? I know I put them in my overcoat pocket...

Oh, it's a bird.

Good morning. How d'you do? Pleased to meet you!

I...er...do forgive me, sir. I'm so absent-minded...Would you believe it: I mistook you for a bird!

Your advertisement reads "Lost: magnificent parrot. Large reward. Finder contact 26 Labrador Road". It will be in tonight's paper, sir.

Ees necesario to make advertisement about the parrot.

There: "Lost: magnificent parrot..." Look, there are two notices. I'll try the first address: it's nearer than the other.

The sooner the better!

Grrreat greedy-guts!

RRRRING

I came about the parrot. Are you the gentleman who...?

Ah, yes! Do come in!

Let's have a look...

It's him all right! I can't thank you enough. You wouldn't believe what he means to me. Please take the reward.

Goodbye, and thank you.

It's me who's grateful!

Now, I want to hear Polly run through his part: "What the parrot saw." But first...

... I need to buy a cage. Look after that box, Snowy. I'll be back in a few minutes...

?

PWARK! PWARK!

GRRREAT GREEDY-GUTS!

?

Who does he think he is?!

Help! They're fighting!... I must be in time to save Polly!

WOOAH GRR PWARK

Grrreat greedy-guts!

Here, have you noticed?...There are two advertisements: and no one has brought back the parrot. It makes me wonder...is someone on the track of of Balthazar's killer?...Anyway, it's an address to remember: 26 Labrador Road.

Si, si...only two people see parrot escape...thees old greedy-guts and thees young man...

Where's that wretched parrot now?

CREAK

CREAK

No doubt about it... there's a burglar in the flat...

Careful... he's in there...

Put your hands up!

9

Ah, it's you!

Caramba! Ees the young man who try to catch the parrot!

Come on! Start talking! You wanted the parrot?

Si! Thees bird he ees mine. You steal heem. I make complain to the policía!

Really? Go right ahead. There's the 'phone; ring the police...

Now, let's be serious. I want to know why you're interested in our feathered friend...

I'm waiting...

WHEEE
THWACK
ZZINNG
? BANG

I saw you were trapped, so I came up quietly and switched off the light.

I have time to throw puñal at heem.

A few inches to the left and ... pfff! Curtains for Tintin! I'll have to watch out; they'll stick at nothing!

I hear the puñal, he go whack into chair. I only miss heem by thees much...

I know, I know ... you need more practice.

That night, at 21 London Road...

BING CRACK CRR

CLACK

That Mr. and Mrs. Dove! They've quarrelled once too often!

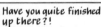

Have you quite finished up there?!

SHUT UP! I AM BALTHAZAR!

HELP! HELP!

Ooh, Colonel! It's the ghost of Mr. Balthazar! I heard his voice! It's him! I know it!

Ghosts? Rubbish! Stuff and nonsense!... We'll see... By the left, quick march!

Close ranks!... Load arms! ...Fix bayonets!

I AM BALTHAZAR!

And I'm Colonel Barker! Surrender! You are surrounded!

Grrreat greedy-guts! ... I am Balthazar!

Faithful unto death: a loving pet! Last night the occupants of 21 London Road, awakened by strange noises, found ...

This time my luck's in! Quick! A taxi! ...

TAXI! ...

TAXI!

I give up. We'll have to walk.

Oh? The parrot? You really are unlucky. The gentleman who bought it yesterday came to collect it again ... Not ten minutes ago...

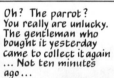

He beat me to it, the gangster. And now he's got the parrot back.

LOOK OUT!

11

Road hog! He couldn't have been closer if he'd tried to run you down!

Yes, he deliberately swerved to the left!

Are you hurt?

No, thanks, I had time to jump clear. I wouldn't have fallen if I hadn't tripped over the edge of the pavement.

I managed to get his number...Wait...169...Yes, 169 MW...That's it. 169 MW... You'll have to ask the police...

169 MW. Thank you!

...I tell you, if that idiot hadn't warned him I'd have settled his hash!

Si, si, but truth ees you meess heem and from now he ees on hees guard. Ciertamente, knife ees better!

In that case, you'll have to practise harder: you always throw too far to the right...

Only a leetle...

That's it... 169 MW... Doctor Eugene Trebblebob, 120 Minstrel's Way... Good!

This time I'm sure I'm on the right track.

MINSTREL'S WAY

Here we are.

169 MW

Wrong number!... That man who told me can't have seen it clearly...

MW 691

Anyway, it's possible they used false number plates on their car... Oh!...

MW 69

EUREKA!

Look, Snowy! You see: 169 MW. Now watch: one... two...

Three!...Presto! ... MW 691!

They just turned their numberplates upside down... Perfectly simple!

Now then... MW 691 ...Alonso Perez, engineer, Sunny Bank, Freshfield ... Not far from here to Freshfield... Let's go!

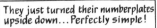

That night...

SUNNY BANK

WHACK

Caramba!... Again ees too much to right!

Ha! ha! ha!... Caramba!... WHOOPEE!

Estúpido parrot! You shut up!

All you need do is aim more to the left: that way you hit the bulls-eye...

Muy bien, aim more to the left?... Why not?

GRRREAT GREEDY-GUTS!

Silencio! Silencio! animal maldito!

Grrreat greedy-guts! Grrreat greedy-guts! PWARK! PWARK!

You!!... You take that!

You fool! What are you doing?...

Carrramba!... Missed again!...

WHACK

Crazy idiot! Think what that parrot means to us! Are you out of your mind? What about the fetish?

Fetish! Fetish! Al infierno weeth thees fetish!... And I wreeng the neck of thees feelthy parrot!...

Calm down, Ramón!

Carrramba! ...Ha! ha! ha!... Grrreat greedy-guts!

Caramba!

Ramón, if you lay a finger on that parrot you're a dead duck!

YEOW!

Mala bestia! Kill heem!

Carrramba!... Missed again!...

Rodrigo Tortilla, you've killed me!

Rodrigo Tortilla!

So it was Tortilla!

Lying crook!... Pretending to be a doctor on a study trip to Europe... But all he wanted was to steal the fetish... and the swine succeeded. By getting rid of Balthazar, he thought he'd covered his tracks. But he reckoned without our feathered friend!... I've got his address. I'm going to fix a meeting. He won't suspect anything...

Hello?... Is that the Hotel Liberty? ...May I speak to Mr. Tortilla, please...

Mr. Tortilla?... I'm so sorry, but he's gone, sir... Yes, to South America ...Yes, he went to Le Havre, he sailed at midday... The boat?... It was called "Ville de Lyon"...

That tells me all I need to know...

We're beaten!... There goes Tortilla peacefully sailing away to South America... If only that brainless parrot had talked just one day sooner...

...next bulletin at eleven o'clock... Now here is some late shipping news...

Do we have to keep listening to that wretched radio?

The strike of dockworkers at the French port of Le Havre has spread today. More than a dozen ships are now delayed. Among vessels not expected to sail before midnight tomorrow is the "Ville de Lyon", bound for South America...

Caramba! All is not lost, Ramón: we have time to get there!

Now, clever Señor Tortilla, the fun begins!

Several days later...

Well? Still nothing?

Nothing. No sign of heem anywhere!

Perhaps he see us and he keep to hees cabin... Or maybe he nevaire come aboard thees ship... Een thees case...

Ssh! Someone's coming...

Did you see?...

That feegure... eet could be...

Tintin, couldn't it?

No, ciertamente ees impossible! ... Also, how could he know?

Sssh!

Or him?

It's crazy! We've started seeing Tintins around every corner! They're all fairly short... O.K.... But what does that prove?

...Ees right.

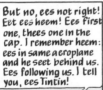

But no, ees not right! Eet ees heem! Ees first one, thees one in the cap. I remember heem: ees in same a croplane and he seet behind us. Ees following us. I tell you, ees Tintin!

All right, there's only one answer. He's got to go!

Esta noche... tonight, after the dinner, we feex heem good!

That evening...

Now don't forget: aim a little more to the left...

Goodnight! ... Oh!

Goodnight to you!

A weeg! Ees wearing a weeg! Ciertamente, ees heem!

Careful, he's coming! Now above all, don't miss!

OOH! ... HELP! ... MURDER! HELP!

STOP THEM!

HELP! HELP! MURDER!

Madre! Ees close theeng... And to think I meess heem as well! ...Ees your fault. You weeth your "Leetle more to the left"!

Well, it's the first time you landed where you aimed... Anyway, it's probably a good thing you didn't hit him, since it wasn't Tintin!

Ees right. But I could swear eet ees heem... Only hees voice when he shout ees not heem.

There's still the other: the little old man.

Next morning...

You are ready? We now go to work weeth thees leetle old man...

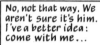

Ees heem!! He spy on us!

O.K., let's see. We'll follow him...

No, not that way. We aren't sure it's him. I've a better idea: come with me...

Get it? If it's Tintin, he must be wearing a false beard. So...

ZZZZ ZZZ

ZZZ ZZ

Steady!... You're nearly there ... A little to the right... Gently... Back a bit... That's it!... Now!

No, it isn't Tintin!

Now we're sure Tintin isn't aboard we can really get down to finding Tortilla...

...weeth fetish!

Ah, there's our steward... Will you join us for a drink?

Thanks...I see you're up bright and early. Not like some I could mention...Take your fellow countryman in cabin 17...Never shows his nose outside the door...

Why not?

Sick?

He says he is, but I don't believe a word of it. Anyway, he hasn't left his cabin since he sailed... Has all his meals there... Well, cheers!

Cheers!

You heard that? The passenger in 17...

And you'll never believe it... Just between the three of us ...the passenger...isn't a man isn't a woman...but...an omelette!

?

?

?

Ha! ha! ha! Now wait for it... D'you know why?... Because he's called Tortilla, and in Spanish tortilla means...

...an omelette! Ha! ha! ha! That's rich!

Ees beeg joke!...

Got to go now... If the Captain sees me here I'll catch it...And you wouldn't want to drop me in the drink, eh?

Get away with you... you're a real caution!

That was a good one...drop in the drink...Get it?

Thanks to that nitwit we've found Tortilla... Ramón, the fetish is ours!

At last!

That night...

SPLASH

Next morning the ship arrives off Las Dopicos, capital of the Republic of San Theodoros, South America

Have you heard?...That Tortilla... He's disappeared! He must have been pushed overboard! There'd been a struggle in his cabin!

How shocking!... Do they know who did it?

They do indeed, gentlemen!...Come on now!...Get your hands up... fast!

Caramba! It's Tintin! I might have known!

Keep a close watch on them till the police arrive...

I am Colonel Jimenez, regular army.

Captain Maldemer...I have two prisoners I'd like to hand over, Colonel.

These two?...I know them both...dangerous crooks, wanted by our police.

Good idea of yours to meet the boat... Excellent... But there's still the fetish...

Don't worry... they won't have it for long!

...And that's the whole story. Look, here's the fetish they stole from the wretched Tortilla. Does anything in particular strike you about it?

I reckon it's another fake. The right ear isn't broken.

Exactly. So we still need to know two things. First, where's the real fetish... and then, what are all these gangsters really after?

RAT TAT TAT

Come in!

A letter for Mr. Tintin, sir. A police launch just brought it.

Republic of San Theodoros
Ministry of Justice
Los Dopicos

The Minister presents his compliments to Mr. Tintin and requests his presence ashore to assist in the interrogation of two suspects. Mr. Tintin is further invited to bring with him the stolen fetish. An officer will meet Mr. Tintin on shore and put himself at his disposal.

Things are beginning to move. I'll just get myself ready and then I'll go.

See you later! Good luck!

Thanks. goodbye.

Don't forget, we'll be sailing tonight at eight o'clock.

Don't worry, I'll be back. I don't want to get stuck in this place!

All right then, that's understood. You'll pick me up here at 1900 hours.

Yes, sir.

Now we just have to wait for that obliging officer to come and put himself at my disposal!

Hey! My suitcase!

Ah!... It's still there... Whew!

What a fright!

That's him, isn't it?

Yes, he's the one!

Will you come with us, señor?...

Ah, there you are. Excellent.

Why all the soldiers every-where?

There's talk of a revolution...

CUARTEL DE SAN JUAN V

tell m... you will find... in harbour. He has with him a small white dog. If you don't believe this letter, open his case...

xxx

RAT TAT TAT

Come in!

This is the man, Captain.

Good. Open your case!

Captain, I don't know whether you're fully in the picture... I was sent for by the Minister of Justice to help in the interrogation of the two...

Cut out the talk! Do as you're told! I said open your case!

Very well, Captain... but I warn you, I shall complain of your behaviour...

Bombs! My informant was right: he's a terrorist!

Hold him! Take him to the cell block at once... to await the firing squad!

Captain, it's all a trick, I tell you! My case was stolen, and switched with this one!

OK, OK, we know all that! To the cells!

Well, well, here I am again... in the soup!

Still, it's not so bad. The launch from the "Ville de Lyon" is due to pick me up at seven. When I don't appear they'll go back to the ship and alert the Captain... He'll get me out easily enough.

Doesn't that dog belong to the lad they just took in?

Yes, and I guess he'll have a long wait for his master...

1900 hours...

Perdone, señor teniente, but are you waiting for a young man to take out to the "Ville de Lyon"?

Yes, how d'you know that?

Because he said to tell you not to wait for him. And here's a letter he asked me to give you...

"To the Captain of the Ville de Lyon." All right, thank you.

That's that taken care of!

There's the launch going back. They'll warn the Captain.

...And there's the letter the man gave me.

Las Dopicos

Dear Captain,
    As you know, I planned to continue my trip with you.
    However, something new has come up concerning the theft of the fetish, forcing me to stay longer in Las Dopicos.
    I am extremely sorry if I have incon-

What's happening? It must be nearly eight o'clock and the launch still isn't back...

TOOOOT TOOOT

That's the "Ville de Lyon"!

They're weighing anchor... sailing without me!!

This time it's hopeless... I can't see any way to get myself off the hook...

And next morning...

Squad!... Ready!...

Take aim...

Stop! Don't shoot!

Hello? What's up? Have I been reprieved?

Comrades! The revolution has triumphed! General Tapioca has fled, the tyrant is on the run! Our glorious General Alcazar is now in command!

Long live General Alcazar!

¡ Fuera los tiranos !

Down with Tapioca!

¡ Viva la libertad !

In which case, sir, you are free...

That suits me!

Colonel!...Ah, Colonel! At last I've found you!

Now what's going on?

?

What is it Colonel? Have they caught General Tapioca?

Caught him?...You couldn't be more wrong, Colonel!... General Alcazar's troops have surrendered. Alcazar himself has fled the country. General Tapioca is now in command!

Are you sure, Colonel?

Sure as eggs are eggs. I've been looking for you for half an hour to break the news!

Hmm...In that case..

Comrades! The rebellion is crushed! General Alcazar has fled, the tyrant is on the run! Let us all swear allegiance to our glorious General Tapioca!

Long live General Tapioca!

Down with Alcazar!

¡ Fuera los tiranos !

¡ Viva la libertad !

I'm terribly sorry, sir, but the way things are, I'll have to carry out my orders and shoot you.

!

Take aim ...

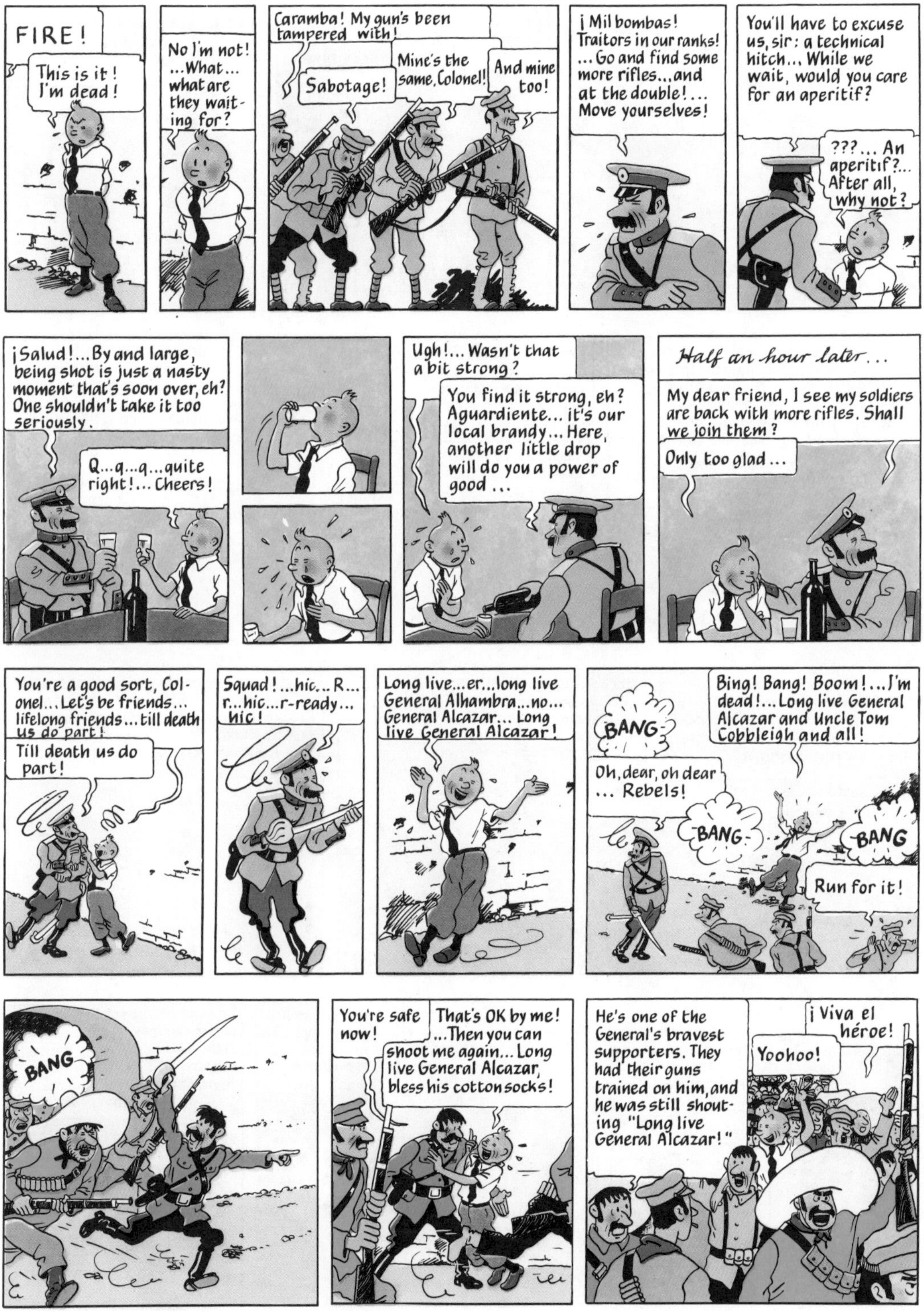
FIRE!
This is it! I'm dead!
No I'm not! ...What... what are they waiting for?
Caramba! My gun's been tampered with!
Sabotage!
Mine's the same, Colonel!
And mine too!
¡Mil bombas! Traitors in our ranks! ...Go and find some more rifles...and at the double!... Move yourselves!
You'll have to excuse us, sir: a technical hitch... While we wait, would you care for an aperitif?
???... An aperitif?... After all, why not?
¡Salud!...By and large, being shot is just a nasty moment that's soon over, eh? One shouldn't take it too seriously.
Q...q...q...quite right!... Cheers!
Ugh!... Wasn't that a bit strong?
You find it strong, eh? Aguardiente... it's our local brandy... Here, another little drop will do you a power of good...
Half an hour later...
My dear friend, I see my soldiers are back with more rifles. Shall we join them?
Only too glad...
You're a good sort, Colonel... Let's be friends... lifelong friends... till death us do part!
Till death us do part!
Squad!...hic... R... r...hic...r-ready... hic!
Long live...er...long live General Alhambra...no... General Alcazar... Long live General Alcazar!
BANG
Bing! Bang! Boom!...I'm dead!... Long live General Alcazar and Uncle Tom Cobbleigh and all!
Oh, dear, oh dear ... Rebels!
BANG
BANG
Run for it!
BANG
You're safe now!
That's OK by me! ...Then you can shoot me again... Long live General Alcazar, bless his cotton socks!
He's one of the General's bravest supporters. They had their guns trained on him, and he was still shouting "Long live General Alcazar!"
¡Viva el héroe!
Yoohoo!

¡Viva el héroe!

Hooray!

Golly!... Look, there's Tintin!

Go and see what's happening, Colonel...and bring that young man here to me. I want to meet him.

I've already been shot three times...so a fourth time makes no odds to me. I'm used to it.

Here he is, General...he was sentenced to death by General Tapioca. Our men arrived just as the firing squad were going to shoot him. They had their rifles up, and this courageous fellow was still shouting "Long live General Alcazar!"

¡Muy bien! I am General Alcazar, and I need men like you! As a mark of my appreciation, I appoint you colonel aide-de-camp.

Thanks very much ...but I'd like my hand back!

But...don't you think, General, it might be wiser to make him a corporal? We only have forty-nine corporals, whereas there are already three thousand four hundred and eighty-seven colonels. So...

Enough!!

I shall do as I like! I'm in command! But since you consider we are short of corporals I will add to their number. Colonel Diaz, I appoint you corporal!

Yes, General!

Here's your colonel's commission, young man. Now, go and get yourself kitted out. Corporal Diaz here will take you to the tailor.

Jolly old tailor!

A colonel's uniform for our young friend?...Excellent! I had this all ready for Colonel Fernandez, who fled with General Tapioca...He was just the same size... And for yourself?...A corporal's outfit? I have just the thing ...

My career is in ruins. But I'll have my revenge, on you and that confounded General Alcazar!

That night ...

Comrades, we have a new member...an officer who preferred to resign his commission rather than continue to serve a tyrant! He will take the oath.

I swear obedience to the laws of our society. I promise to fight against tyranny with all my strength. My watchword henceforward is the same as yours: liberty or death!

The next morning...

 Where's my new aide-de-camp? Not here yet?

Not yet, General.

 As soon as he arrives send him in. We have work to do...

Very good, sir. At once.

 Colonel!... How on earth did I come to be a colonel? I don't remember a thing...

 However, I'm still looking for the fetish, and to do that I must resign my commission.

 No, gentlemen: impossible. The general is waiting for his ADC. He won't see anyone this morning.

 Them! Heem! Oh!

 Ah, there you are, Colonel. We must get down to work. As for you, gentlemen: I cannot receive you this morning... Come, Colonel!

 No more need for me to resign, for the time being.

The general choose heem! It's crazy!

 Thees ees bad!

Yes, now we'll have to deal with him all over again!

 Meanwhile... His office window is open... So far so good!

 It's a delicate position...

Yes, very delicate.

 I'm sorry, Your Excellency, but the General can't see you this morning. The General is extremely busy...

 Checkmate, my dear Colonel!

Goodness! You're right!

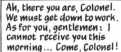

25

My dear Colonel, I shall never forget how you saved my life!

No, General, let's say I managed to save both our lives...

Caramba! Back to square one again!

We've been taken for a ride. The fetish he had in his suitcase was a fake. But he certainly knows where the real one is. So tonight, we'll have him picked up...

And we make heem tell us where the real fetish ees...

That evening...

What a wind!... We're in for a storm tonight...

Look!... He's coming!

HELP! HELP!

Whack! and off he goes to dreamland!

Get off!

An hour later...

That's agreed then: as soon as he's told us where the fetish is, we get rid of him for good!

Ees right: he gives us beeg trouble.

THUMP THUMP THUMP THUMP

Come!

We got him.

Good. Bring him in here...

Welcome to our humble abode, my dear Colonel!...Sit down and have a chat...

A neat trick, Colonel. The idea of putting a fake fetish in your suit-case wasn't bad...But now we'd like to know where the real one is...

Me too... I'd like to know that...

Come on! Cut the funny stuff! Where is it?

I've told you, I don't know.

Ah! Like that, is it? Very well.

I'll give you three minutes to answer my question. After that, a little squeeze with my finger and... click!... Understand?

BOMMM
BRROM
*

Caramba! Ees beeg storm!...

One minute...

If only... if only I could free myself...

Tintin?... What's happened to Tintin?

Ees no use to struggle so hard, amigo. Ees good strong cord and tied very nice. You take my word for that...

Two minutes...

I must tell them something... doesn't matter what it is... otherwise I'm done for.

Thirty seconds to go...

All right. I'll tell you where to find the fetish...

Aha!... I knew we'd come to an understanding in the end. Where is it?

It... er... well, briefly, it's in my trunk aboard the "Ville de Lyon".

Thanks... That's all we wanted you to tell us.

And now we don't need you any more you can say your prayers! You're going to die!

Pronto, pronto, Alonso. You know I am upset by capital punishment...

Quick! He must have gone through the window!...

Down there! Ees trying to reach the road!

He cannot be far away...

There! Spot on! Every time a coconut!

Good old Snowy! There you are!

CÁRCEL

Good morning. I've brought you some customers!

Ten o'clock, and he still isn't here!

Now, quickly, back to the general.

RAT TAT TAT

Come in!

DYNAM

That's it...All I need is a light...

DYNA

DYN

DYNAM

¡Madre! I've forgotten my matches!...

DYNA

Hmm!...Surely I can smell something burning...

DYNA

Caramba! Back to square one again!

Check to your king, General!

Diablo!... I must watch what I'm doing...

That's checkmate, General!

¡Mil millón bombas! You dare to beat me, your general?!

BANG BANG BANG BANG BANG

Ha! ha! ha! ha!

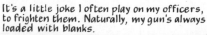

It's a little joke I often play on my officers, to frighten them. Naturally, my gun's always loaded with blanks.

That reminds me of an aide I had a while back. Ha! ha! ha! ha!.. One day, he beat me at chess. I pulled out my gun...

This time, General Alcazar, your reign is at an end! Liberty or death!

DYNA

I pulled out my gun and fired. Ha! ha ha! ... Just imagine, the chap fainted... Ha! ha! ha!... And best of all, can you believe it, next day he had jaundice! ... Imagine! Jaundice!

Justice is done!

An attack!

The general's palace! ...It's over there!

Another revolution?...

It's all right! Quite all right! General Alcazar is unharmed!

Idiot! Surely you know that if you just put dynamite against a wall it only produces a loud bang: you need to bury it...Now, it's back to square one again!

Next morning ...

Hello?... Is that General Alcazar's palace?...Oh, it's you, doctor. How is the general?... What?... What??... JAUNDICE!!!

Jaundice, yes... Caused by shock, you know...

RAT TAT TAT

Come!

Who is it?

R.W. Trickler, representative, General American Oil. All right, show him in.

Good morning. Do please sit down.

Well, Colonel, the reason I'm here... I heard yesterday...

Please excuse me...

Yes, of course...

RRRING

Hello?... Hello?... Yes, Captain... What?!... They've escaped!

We are free, and soon the fetish ees ours!

And soon we'll have our revenge too; we have old scores to settle with Tintin!

Now, sir... I'm all yours...

Well, a geological survey party has just announced evidence of oil deposits in the Gran Chapo region... the desert lying partly in your own country and partly in the neighbouring territory, the Republic of Nuevo-Rico.

General American Oil seeks to obtain a concession to work these fields. Obviously, your government will have an interest in the profits that would accrue...

I see. I'm afraid General Alcazar is ill, and I cannot...

Of course, of course. But you could render us invaluable service. I mentioned that part of the oilfields lie in Nuevo-Rican territory. My company wishes to exploit the whole region: so it follows that you must take over the area.

But... that would mean war!

Unfortunately, yes. But what can one do? You can't make an omelette without breaking eggs, can you, Colonel?

So, here's the reason for my visit. We will give you 100,000 dollars in cash if you will persuade General Alcazar to undertake the campaign... Is it a deal?

?!

You're making a big mistake in refusing my offer. But, just as you wish, Colonel! Goodbye!

A dangerous fellow! He could wreck all our plans. I must have a word with Rodriguez about him...

Yes, Rodriguez, I will offer 10,000 dollars to be rid of him...

If Your Excellency were so kind as to entrust the money to me... I am sure matters could be arranged...

So, that's a deal, Pablo? 5,000 dollars for an accident to happen to Colonel Tintin...

OK. The accident will occur tonight!

Bravo, Ramón! Aim like that tonight and Tintin will be no more than an unpleasant memory!

Caramba! Missed again!

OOOOOOH!

Mercy, señor Colonel! Mercy! I will tell everything...

Ramón! What on earth...? Are you hurt?

What happened? Quick, tell me...

Oooh!...He keell me!...

Here, sit down...

Ooooh!

YEOWW!

Who was it? Who paid you to get rid of me?

It was Rodriguez ...Mr. Trickler's right hand man...

I see...Now get up. I forgive you.

Oh, thank you, thank you, señor Colonel. I am your devoted servant...for life!

I really think he meant it, poor devil!

You shouldn't trust a rascal like that. You're far too gullible!

Some days later...

The General is back: he's completely recovered. At the moment he's talking to Mr. Trickler.

Look, General... just think... It's wholly to your advantage. As I say, you declare war on Nuevo-Rico, and you annexe the oilfields. My company makes a profit on the oil and your country gets 35% But naturally you deduct 10% for personal expenses...

Yes...very neat...I accept.

Excellent, General. I was sure we would understand one another.

By the way, General...that Colonel Tintin, in whom you seem to have so much confidence...Let me give you some advice: don't trust him. I won't say any more now...

Good morning, my dear Colonel...The General awaits you...

Good morning, General. I'm glad to see you're better. I...

What is it now?

!?! He doesn't seem in a very good mood today...

Send him in.

Basil Bazarov

KORRUPT ARMS GMBH

Good morning, General Alcazar. I happened to be passing through your country, and thought I'd show you our latest models.

This is our very newest line: the 75 TRGP. It's a really high-quality product: flexible, easy to handle, strong, and it will toss a nice little nickel-plated shell for you over a distance of 15 kilometres.

75 TRGP

GRENADE

Oho! This could be serious. Listen, Ramón. Las Dopicos. A detachment of Nuevo-Rican soldiers crossed into the territory of San Theodoros and opened fire on a border post. Guards returned the fire and a violent battle ensued. The Nuevo-Ricans were forced to retire across the frontier, having sustained heavy losses. The only casualty on our side was a corporal, wounded by a cactus spine.

The airport...

Now we are off to San-facion... the Nuevo-Rican capital.

Very good, sir.

LAS DOPICOS

...and six dozen 75 TRGP, with 60,000 shells, for the government of San Theodoros. Payable in twelve monthly instalments.

SANFACION

To General Mogador's palace.

Very good, señor.

Half an hour later...

Back to the airport.

Si, señor.

That's Señor Bazarov's private plane

SANFACION

...and six dozen 75 TRGP, with 60,000 shells, for the government of Nuevo-Rico. Payment in twelve monthly instalments.

Here he comes, back already to Las Dopicos

Well?

All done. Another fat order...and something to fix Colonel Tintin too!

Now pay attention. It's a time bomb, with a clock. It's set to explode at exactly eleven o'clock tomorrow morning...And you'd better succeed this time!

I'll succeed, chief! Liberty or death!

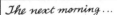

The next morning...

General, I warned you against Colonel Tintin... Look at this letter and tell me if I was wrong...

REPUBLIC OF NUEVO-RICO

★★★

WAR OFFICE   SECRET

Dear Colonel Tintin,

We have safely received the plans of the 75 TRGP which the government of San Theodoros has just acquired.

As promised, the agreed fee will now be paid to you.

X.14

A spy!... ¡Mil bombas! Planted as a spy!...The traitor!... The rat!... He'll pay dearly for this!

Hello!...Hello!...Colonel Juanitos?...Take ten men and go and arrest Colonel Tintin at once!...Eh? What? ...That's an order, Colonel! ...Move!

Meanwhile...

The explosion is set for 11 a.m. ... What's the time? ...Hello, my watch has stopped!

Now, let's put it right...

CALLE DEL SOL

Come in!

RAT TAT TAT

Good morning, Colonel Juanitos. Good to see you...

I'm terribly sorry, Colonel Tintin, but I've been ordered to arrest you!

Arrest me?... Me??...

There's been a power cut this morning, so all the municipal clocks have stopped. Go and put them right.

Ten o'clock. There's still some time before I need to deposit my little box of fireworks!

Ah, General Alcazar, you're going to repent making me a corporal! Insult me at your peril! Corporal Diaz takes his revenge!

CALLE DE ALCALA

Yes, you can take these: they're my orders. The first concerns Colonel Tintin; he will be shot at dawn tomorrow. The other is for Corporal Diaz, my former aide-de-camp. I've made him a colonel again. He can resume his duties at once.

BOOM

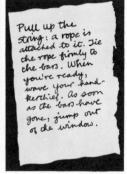

Back in gaol again! Unless I'm much mistaken, friend Trickler has cooked this one up to get rid of me.

Oh!... It won't be easy to escape...

Nightfall, and I still can't see any way out...There must be something...

Pull up the string: a rope is attached to it. Tie the rope firmly to the bars. When you're ready, wave your handkerchief. As soon as the bars have gone, jump out of the window.

Ah, here comes the rope ...

That's it: he's signalling! Pull!

!

Hello?

Come on, jump! Quick!

Follow me! Hurry! They've raised the alarm.

Pablo, I'll never forget what you've done for me!

Come...Quickly!

Take no notice! They shoot like a bunch of drunks!

There. Take the car and go. By midday tomorrow you'll be over the frontier. Don't worry about me: I've covered my tracks. I shan't have any trouble. Goodbye, señor Tintin.

Goodbye, dear Pablo. I shall remember...

It is nothing, señor. I haven't forgotten that day you spared my life!

Hello?... What? ¡Mil millón bombas!...!?¿i... Recapture him, or I'll shoot every guard at the prison!

I can't just run them over ...I'll stop, and play it carefully...

Perfect! They've moved out of the way! On we go!

?!?

Caramba! It was him!

Tintin went past in a car...heading south!

I want him, dead or alive!

Next morning, at dawn...

There!!

It's him!... Open fire!

RAT TAT TAT TAT

Snakes! I'm being followed!

CRACK

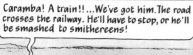

?

TOOOOOOT

Caramba! A train!!...We've got him. The road crosses the railway. He'll have to stop, or he'll be smashed to smithereens!

Tintin, my friend, this time it's all or nothing...

He's going...!!

The fool!

Whew!

We cut things a bit fine there... eh, Snowy?

Now, step on the gas! We'll get him in the mountains.

Mountains! That's bad. Their car's much more powerful, and they'll soon catch us up...

Tintin! You'll kill us!

He went over...

Caramba! What a drop!

I'm staying here. Why climb down ? He's had it anyway, hasn't he?

As you like. I'm going to see...

There it is. We can go back to Las Dopicos. That's put paid to Colonel Tintin.

VRROOM

What's going on up there ?

?

That's our car !

!

He...he must have been hiding behind the rocks. I didn't see him coming...

It doesn't matter. He'll be caught at the frontier. It can't be far from here. We'll pick him up there. Come on !

?

It's a government car !

If they stop me, I'm caught... and if that's a strong barrier, I'm dead.

PAAAARP

CRACK

!

Hello?... Border post 31?... Patrol No. 4 here... A San-Theodorian car with a mounted machine-gun just raced past here, heading for the frontier.

Red alert!... San-Theodorian armoured car reported... Man your posts!

?

RATATATAT

Watch out, Snowy!... They're shooting at our tyres!

An armoured car tried to attack border post 31. It was destroyed and one of the occupants, a colonel, was taken prisoner.

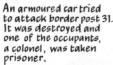

In Sanfacion...

General!...General!...This dispatch has just come by telephone!

"An armoured car ..."!!! This time it's war! That's what they want: that's what they'll get!

Pass this communiqué to the newspapers. I want special editions on the streets in an hour!

Sanfacion Star! ...Extra!...Extra!... Sanfacion Star! ..., Extra!

WAR! IT'S WAR! A motorised column of the San-Theodorian army mounted a surprise attack today, but the enemy were repulsed by our valiant troops, who inflicted heavy casualties...

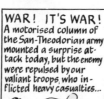

LAS DOPICOS HERE WE COME!

ALCAZAR OUT!

DEATH TO ALCAZAR

Hello?...Mr.Trickler? ...Success! The Nuevo-Ricans have just declared war on us!...Yes...over some new incident on the border...

The Gran Chapo fields are ours!!... Once again General American Oil has beaten British South-American Petrol!!

In a fortnight all the Gran Chapo will be in Nuevo-Rican hands. Then I hope you in British South-American Petrol will not forget your promises.

The first chance we get, we desert, and...

...we look for thees fetish again.

Meanwhile...

What will happen to me?

I don't know. We've been ordered to take you to Sanfacion, and that's all.

Good old Snowy! ... Keep on chewing!

Free!

This is it! Out we go!

BANG
BANG

WOUT

BANG
BANG

BANG

WOOAAAH!

SPLOSH

Hold your fire: he's out of range. Let him go. He'll be swept over the falls...

If I can't reach that rock, I'm done for!

Whew!

WOOAH!

Well, what do we do now?

?

A tree trunk!... Don't let it go ... it could be our only chance!

Ah! It's swinging round!

That's it...We can get across... with luck!

We're safe now, Snowy.

The first thing is to find out where we are...

Meanwhile...

Caramba! Listen to this, Ramon...

Drama at sea. The liner 'Ville de Lyon' caught fire last night in mid-ocean. Agency reports state that passengers and crew are safe, but all cargo and baggage have been destroyed.

The fetish! The fetish burnt!

Unless...unless thees Tintin is lying when he tell us thees fetish is in hees trunk...

A house, at long last!

He's lost, and is seeking shelter?...But of course, bring him in...

Don José Trujillo owns this hacienda...He is very happy to welcome you.

That evening...

So the river is the Coliflor?... Don't the Arumbayas live somewhere along the banks of the Coliflor?

Yes, they do. But there aren't many who'd dare go that way. The Arumbayas are the fiercest Indians in the whole of South America. The last man to try was a British explorer, Ridgewell. He went more than ten years ago. He's never been seen since.

Oh!

D'you think there's anyone who'd agree to take me there?

?

This is Caraco, an Indian who knows the river well. But I doubt if he'd dare go... there.

I want to go down-river. Will you act as my guide?

Si, señor.

I ... er... I want to visit the Arumbayas ...

!

Arumbayas! Very bad people! No! Caraco no go!

Chicken!

Wait, Caraco. Think it over. Look what I'll pay you ...

Caraco go. But Caraco very poor man. The señor will buy canoe of Caraco.

All right, I'll buy it.

Caraco know other white señor. He want to go to Arumbayas. Long, long time ago. Other white señor ...

I know, he never came back...

And that doesn't bother you?

Several days later...

Soon is night, señor.

You're right. We must stop.

Tomorrow, we come to country of Arumbayas.

Goodnight, señor...

Goodnight, Caraco.

Next morning...

Where's Caraco?

The canoe is still there, anyway ...

He's left me!...Now I understand why he wanted me to buy his canoe... So I could go on alone!

Careful now!... Rapids!

The canoe!...The canoe, with the guns and the food!... All gone!

Well! Now I really am in a jam! ...No gun, no food, in hostile country...and all by myself!

!?!...I don't count any more, I suppose?

It's funny, but I have a feeling somebody's watching us...

Y...y... you...th-th-think...s-so?

OH!

A dart!.., It's sure to be poisoned!... D'you remember, Snowy?...Curare!

I can't hear anything now. I must have shaken them off...

Cowards! Come on out and show yourselves, unless you're afraid to!

Tintin, you'll get yourself killed!

WOOAH

!

Great snakes!

A white man!

Who are you? And what brings you to this place?

My name is Tintin... who... who are you?

My name is Ridgewell.

Ridgewell? The explorer? But everybody thinks you're dead.

What a pity! Or rather, what a good thing, because I've decided never to return to civilisation. I'm happy here among the Arumbayas, whose life I share...

And whose weapons you've adopted. What was the meaning of that little game of darts?

I just wanted you to have an un-friendly reception, to encourage you to leave at once. Believe me, if I'd wanted to kill you it wouldn't have taken more than one dart. Look, I'll prove it. You see that big flower over there?

Yes.

Good shot!

WOOAAAAH!

?

Ooh! I'm so sorry!

WOOAAAH!

Don't worry, the dart wasn't poisoned. Use my hand-kerchief for a bandage.

Now, tell me how you come to be here in this country...

Well, it's like this. An Arumbaya fetish in a museum in Europe, brought back by the explorer Walker, was stolen and replaced by a copy. I noticed the substitution. Two other men were also on the track of the real fetish and who-ever had stolen it.

I followed these two men to South America. They killed the thief on board ship and stole his fetish. But this one too was a fake. So now I'm trying to find the real fetish, and I still don't know where it is.

...Just as I still don't know what they were all after: Tortilla, the first thief, and his two killers. They all want-ed the fetish. But why they wanted it is still a complete mystery. So I thought perhaps that here...

...among the Arumbayas I might learn something fresh about it...

Perhaps you may. It's quite possible...

Rumbabas! ...Sworn enemies of the Arumbayas! ...

What will they do to us? That's easy! They'll cut off our heads and by a most ingenious process they'll shrink them to the size of an apple!

Ahw wada lu'vali bahn chaco conats! Ha! ha! ha!

Just as I thought. He means our heads will soon be added to his collection!

They've gone...Snowy, you've absolutely got to save Tintin.

If I can find the Arumbaya village, and take this thing to them, perhaps they'll understand that its owner is in danger...

Meanwhile, in the Arumbaya village...

The Spirits tell me that if your son is to be cured, he must eat the heart of the first animal you meet in the forest...

I go, most powerful one!

What a strange animal!...And what's it carrying in its mouth? A quiver! That's funny...I must try to catch it alive...

See, O witch-doctor. This cloth belongs to the old bearded one, and the quiver also. Perhaps the old bearded one is in danger?

You mind your own business!...Give me the animal and go!...I shall kill the creature and take out its heart; this I shall give to your son to eat. Go now!

And if you breathe one word of all this, I shall call the Spirits upon you and your family...and you will all be changed into frogs!

No danger now: he won't gossip...But he's right. The old bearded one may be in trouble. All the better! Let's hope he dies! Then I shall regain my power over the Arumbayas. Now, before I kill the animal I must burn these things...they might give me away.

Great Spirits of the forest, we bring thee a sacrifice of these two strangers...

Stop, O chief of the Rumbabas! The Spirits of the forest do not accept your sacrifice!

These two strangers are friends of the forest. You will set them free.

V-v-very w-w-w-... well!

It's magic... witchcraft!

Magic?... Didn't you realise it was me speaking?...I'm a ventriloquist... Ventriloquism, I'd have you know my young friend, is my pet hobby.

Good heavens!

Brother Arumbayas, you are about to witness a remarkable phenomenon...

My end!

We will take out this animal's heart and give it, still beating, to our sick brother...

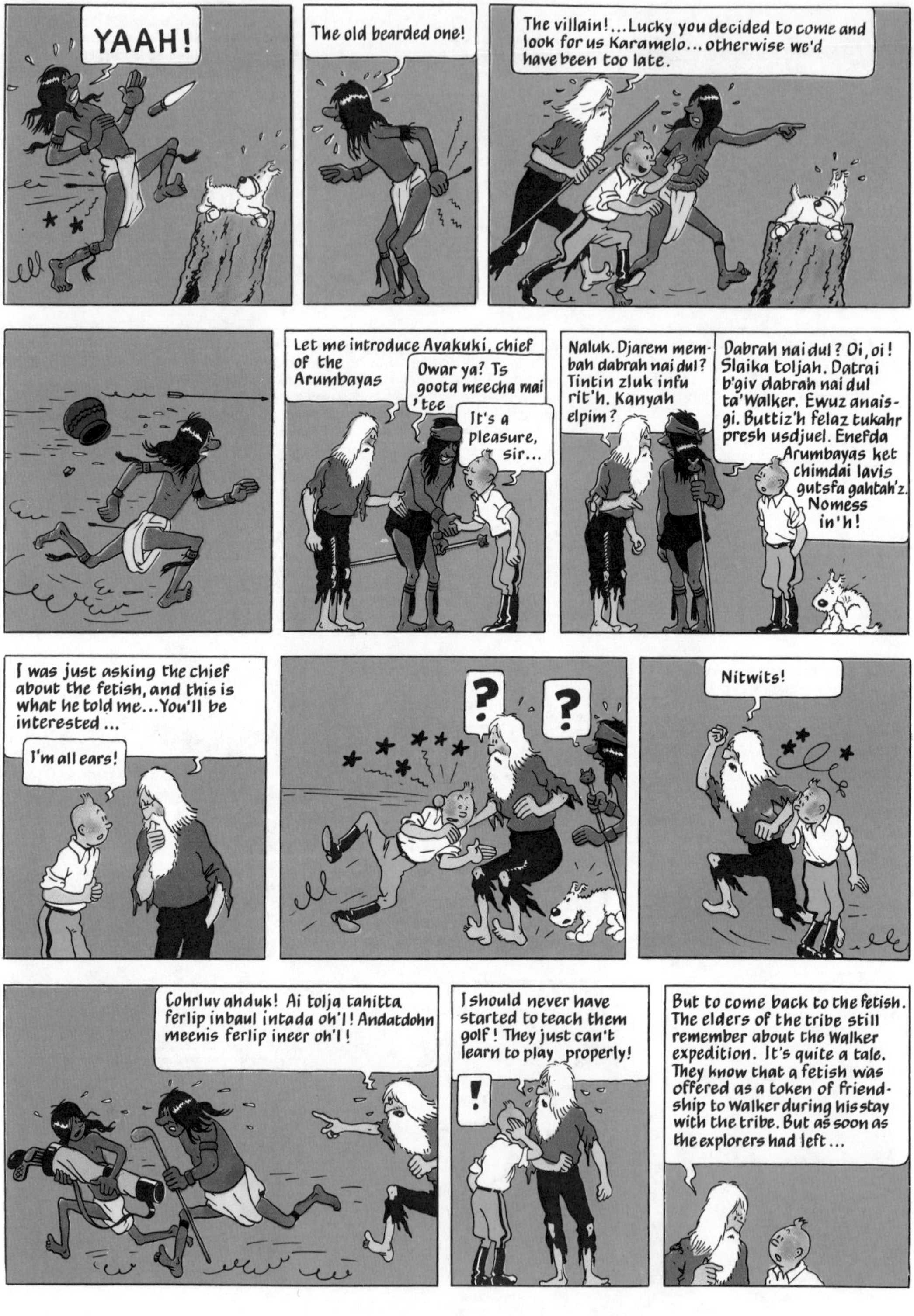
YAAH!
The old bearded one!
The villain!...Lucky you decided to come and look for us Karamelo... otherwise we'd have been too late.
Let me introduce Avakuki, chief of the Arumbayas
Owar ya? Ts goota meecha mai 'tee
It's a pleasure, sir...
Naluk. Djarem membah dabrah nai dul? Tintin zluk infu rit'h. Kanyah elpim?
Dabrah nai dul? Oi, oi! Slaika toljah. Datrai b'giv dabrah nai dul ta'Walker. Ewuz anaisgi. Buttiz'h felaz tukahr presh usdjuel. Enefda Arumbayas ket chimdai lavis gutsfa gahtah'z. Nomess in'h!
I was just asking the chief about the fetish, and this is what he told me... You'll be interested...
I'm all ears!
?
?
Nitwits!
Cohrluv ahduk! Ai tolja tahitta ferlip inbaul intada oh'l! Andatdohn meenis ferlip ineer oh'l!
I should never have started to teach them golf! They just can't learn to play properly!
!
But to come back to the fetish. The elders of the tribe still remember about the Walker expedition. It's quite a tale. They know that a fetish was offered as a token of friendship to Walker during his stay with the tribe. But as soon as the explorers had left...

The Arumbayas discovered that a sacred stone had disappeared. It seems that the stone gave protection from snake-bite to anyone who touched it. The tribe remembered a half-caste named Lopez, the explorers' interpreter, who was often seen prowling around the hut where the magic sto-e was kept under guard.

The Arumbayas were furious. They set off in pursuit of the expedition, caught up with them, and massacred almost all the party... Walker himself managed to escape, carrying the fetish. As for the half-caste, although badly wounded, he too got away. The stone, probably a diamond, was never recovered... That's how the story goes.

Now I understand... The whole thing makes sense!

Listen!... The half-caste steals the stone, and to avoid suspicion he conceals it in the fetish. He thinks he'll be able to get it back later on...

But the Arumbayas attack the expedition and Lopez is wounded. He has to flee without the diamond. And that's it!... The diamond is still in its hiding-place, and that's why Tortilla, and after him his two killers, tried to steal the fetish.

It looks to me as if you're right!

So now all I have to do is find the fetish... and return to Europe!

Some days later...

Meanwhile...

REPUBLIC OF SAN THEODOROS
NOTICE
DESERTERS
ALONSO PERF.
RAMON BADA

We simply must get hold of a canoe...

Look!... There ees canoe ... and weeth one man only... But... I theenk I am seeing theengs... or ees a dream... Thees man...

Caramba!... It's Tintin!

We'll rest here for a while before we continue our journey...

So we meet again, eh?

?

Let's start talking!... Did you know the 'Ville de Lyon' had been completely destroyed by fire... burnt out!

Really?

Yes, really! And the fetish you left in your trunk has been destroyed!...Burnt!... All because of you...You are going to pay dearly, my friend!

No! I told you...The real fetish wasn't aboard...

Oho! So you lied to us! Well, now you're going to tell us where it is. And don't try to fool us again!

I've already told you: I know nothing about it...

Now listen carefully! There's one more round left in this gun. On the count of three if you haven't talked, I swear that bullet's for you! One!...two!...

Look out! A snake!!!...

Where?

YOW!

Here!

OOH!

!?

Caramba!!!

Ha! ha! ha! I've got you at last!...

Good!... Now they're safely taken care of, let's see what he's got in his wallet.

OHO!

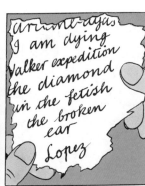
Arrumbayas I am dying Valker expedition the diamond in the fetish the broken ear Lopez

Where did you get this note?... Tell me!

In the ship, on our way to Europe. Tortilla dropped it. But we didn't know what it meant. Tortilla was just a fellow passenger. We only realised the significance of the paper when we read about the fetish being stolen from the museum...Then we decided we'd try to get the fetish away from Tortilla.

Excellent!... Now, the only thing we don't know is how Tortilla got hold of this note. But since he's dead, I don't suppose we'll ever discover that!...So now, gentlemen, let's get moving!

And behave yourselves!

What are you planning to do with us?

No problem. I shall hand you over to justice. I think you well deserve it!

Hand us over to justice?... Ha! ha! ha!

!

Don't count your chickens before they're hatched, my fine friend...

?

Teep heem een!...

Got you!

Bravo!

There!...

Hee's feenished! Look, Alonso. Thees piranhas, thees man-eating feeshes... they come for heem already

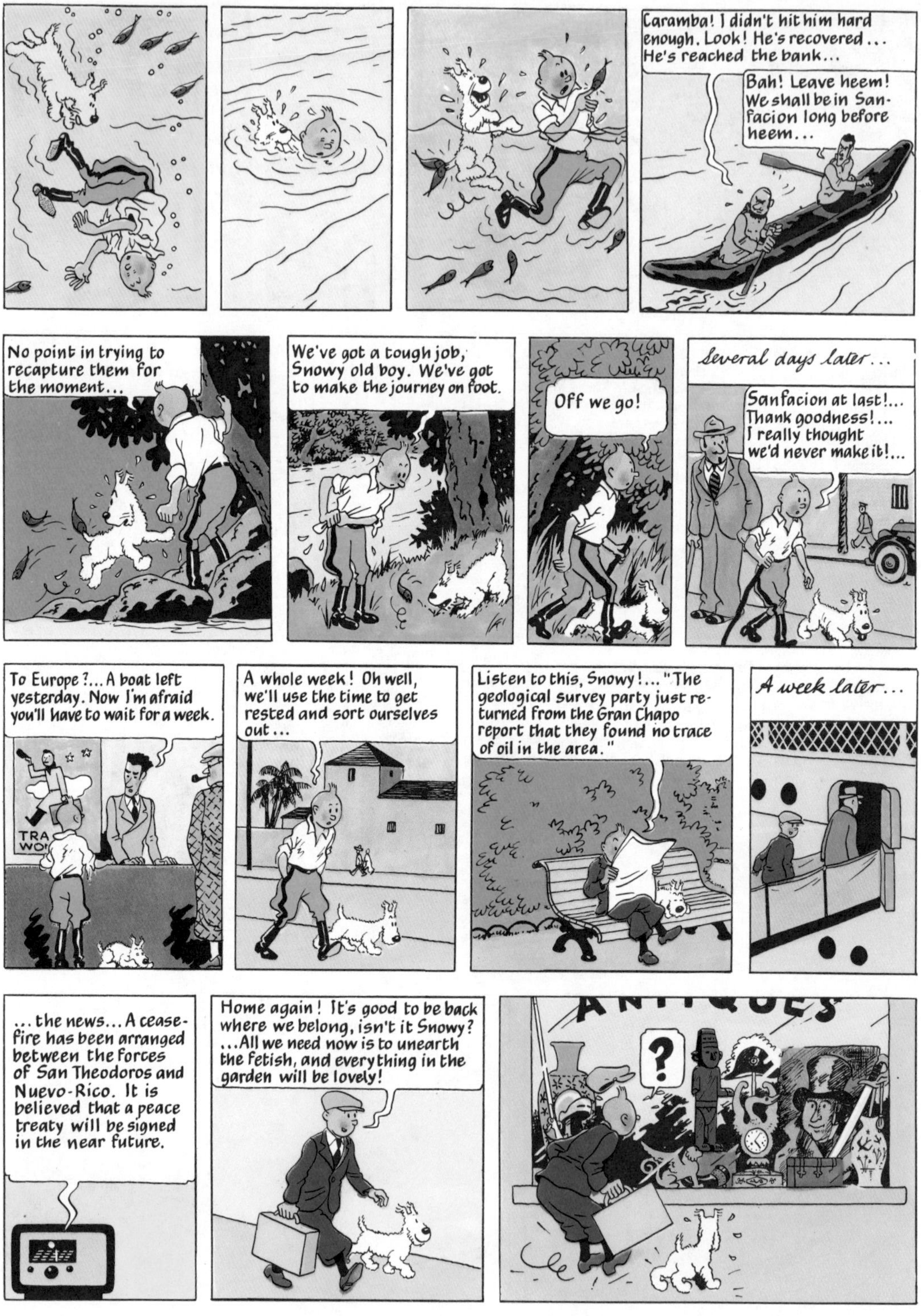
Caramba! I didn't hit him hard enough. Look! He's recovered ... He's reached the bank...
Bah! Leave heem! We shall be in Sanfacion long before heem...
No point in trying to recapture them for the moment...
We've got a tough job, Snowy old boy. We've got to make the journey on foot.
Off we go!
Several days later...
Sanfacion at last!... Thank goodness!... I really thought we'd never make it!...
To Europe ?... A boat left yesterday. Now I'm afraid you'll have to wait for a week.
TRA
WO
A whole week! Oh well, we'll use the time to get rested and sort ourselves out...
Listen to this, Snowy!... "The geological survey party just returned from the Gran Chapo report that they found no trace of oil in the area."
A week later...
... the news... A cease-fire has been arranged between the forces of San Theodoros and Nuevo-Rico. It is believed that a peace treaty will be signed in the near future.
Home again! It's good to be back where we belong, isn't it Snowy? ...All we need now is to unearth the fetish, and everything in the garden will be lovely!
ANTIQUES
?

Good heavens!... It's fantastic!

Think of the thousands of miles I've travelled to find this thing!

£100...Cheap at the price!... But come to think of it, I should have asked how he managed to get hold of the fe........tish...

?*!?**!?*

£17.50 THE PAIR

!?!...There's no mistake... They've both got a broken ear! ...I can't believe it... It's absolutely incredible!

This time I really will find out where they came from!

Good morning. Would you be kind enough to tell me who brought you those two fetishes?

Ah, yes, the two little fetishes... who brought them to me?...

A bit of a struggle, but at last I've got the address...Mr. Balthazar, 32 Lamb's Lane...That isn't very far. We'll go straight there.

J. BALTHAZAR

32

This is it.

OFFICES AND WORKSHOPS

Here we are...

OFFICES AND WORKSHOPS

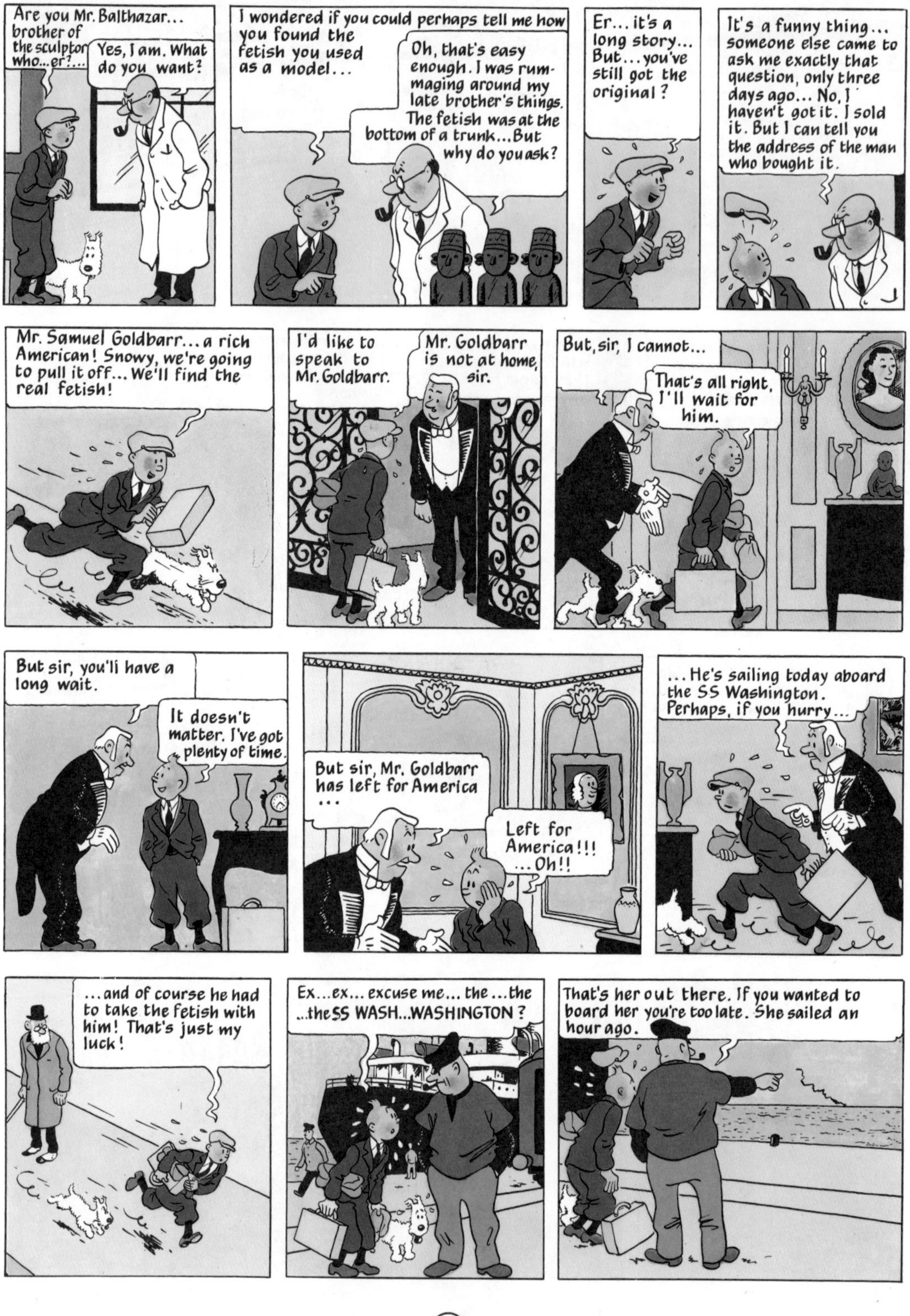
Are you Mr. Balthazar... brother of the sculptor who...er?...
Yes, I am. What do you want?
I wondered if you could perhaps tell me how you found the fetish you used as a model...
Oh, that's easy enough. I was rummaging around my late brother's things. The fetish was at the bottom of a trunk...But why do you ask?
Er... it's a long story... But... you've still got the original?
It's a funny thing... someone else came to ask me exactly that question, only three days ago... No, I haven't got it. I sold it. But I can tell you the address of the man who bought it.
Mr. Samuel Goldbarr... a rich American! Snowy, we're going to pull it off... We'll find the real fetish!
I'd like to speak to Mr. Goldbarr.
Mr. Goldbarr is not at home, sir.
But, sir, I cannot...
That's all right, I'll wait for him.
But sir, you'll have a long wait.
It doesn't matter. I've got plenty of time.
But sir, Mr. Goldbarr has left for America ...
Left for America!!! ...Oh!!
... He's sailing today aboard the SS Washington. Perhaps, if you hurry...
...and of course he had to take the fetish with him! That's just my luck!
Ex...ex... excuse me... the ...the ...the SS WASH...WASHINGTON?
That's her out there. If you wanted to board her you're too late. She sailed an hour ago.

But if you really want to catch her, maybe you could hitch a ride from the air-base over there ... It's not far ...

...catch the 'Washington', eh? ... Hmm...maybe... We happen to have a plane going out to her... to deliver some mail ...

First service for lunch, please! ...First service for lunch! ...

There goes Goldbarr... He's off to lunch. Now's our chance!

Ramón!... Ramón!... Look!... I've got it!

Here comes the mail...

But the diamond ...Where is it?

Eet must be somewhere inside...

Leesten, Alonso...We cannot stay here any longer. Ees too reesky. Someone might come. We take thees fetish to our cabin, then we take our time to look...

Hello...there's a passenger...

I need to speak to one of your passengers immediately... A Mr. Goldbarr...

Mr. Goldbarr? You'll find him in the first-class dining-room.

Let's hope I've come in time!

!

?

TINTIN!

Hands up!...

OH!

The diamond!

Look out! Thees diamond!

It'll go into the sea!

Ees lost!...Ees because of you... You, pay for thees!

AAH! WOOAH BANG BANG HELP!

Three men overboard, sir!...

?!

Someone said there were three of them...

Look!...They're fishing one out now...

The...the others?...
...Went straight on down!

Oooh! My fetish! My beautiful fetish!

Mr. Goldbarr?...I'm terribly sorry your fetish has been damaged. I can explain everything if you'll allow me...

...I think you should know that your fetish is stolen property.

Stolen?! ...But I...

Yes, I know where you bought it, and I'm sure the man who sold it to you acted in good faith...

If that's the case, I wouldn't consider keeping the fetish for a moment longer. If you're going back on shore, can I ask you to take it and restore it to the museum where it belongs? I'd be greatly obliged!

OF ETHNOGR

May I please speak to the Director?

And now, Snowy my friend, we're going to take a well-earned rest!

Wooah! Wooah!

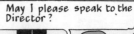

Toreador, on guard now! Torea- dor! Toreador!

HERGÉ

THE ADVENTURES OF TINTIN

THE BLACK ISLAND

THE BLACK ISLAND

A plane in trouble?

PFTT PFTT PFTT

Sounds bad.

It's probably a private aircraft.

Let's see, Snowy.

Will it take long to fix?

No, only a few minutes. Nothing seriously wrong.

Why, it's an unregistered plane.

Someone coming, Mick.

Too bad for him! You know our orders.

Are you in trouble? Can I help?

Next morning...

Well, doctor? He was lucky. The bullet only grazed a rib. He'll be up and about in a couple of days.

Excuse me, nurse.

Can we see Tintin, please?

You can go in.

Look here: are you absolutely sure the plane had no registration marks?

Quite certain.

It all looks very fishy to me.

To be precise: the whole thing looks like me, very fishy.

Telephone, please, for Mr Thomson or Mr Thompson.

Hello?...Yes... Interpol?...Yes sir, Thompson, with a p, as in psychology... From Scotland Yard?... Eastdown? Last night?...Yes sir, I understand. We'll leave at once.

We're going back to England. An unregistered plane crashed last night near a place called Eastdown, in Sussex. Goodbye.

Goodbye, and watch your step!

Thanks!

CRASH

Why can't you look where you're going?

To be precise: speak for yourself.

Eastdown... If only... It can't be helped, I simply must go. Never mind doctor's orders!

Goodbye, nurse. Many thanks!

Ach! The silly fools! Who d'you think they shot at last night? Tintin himself! Pity they didn't finish him off while they were about it.

Look!!

Why have we stopped?

Let's look in the corridor.

There's a door open, and someone's getting out. Come on, Snowy!

There he goes!

What d'you think you're doing?

Eek!

Let me go! A man just jumped off the train. We must follow him!

You can't fool me.

Everybody stay where you are!

No one is to leave the train.

He's coming round.

Tintin! Aren't you in bed?

There he is! I'd know him anywhere. He knocked me out!

Me??

Aha! A cosh! Useful for knocking people on the head.

Robbery, too! Here's the poor man's wallet, in your other pocket.

I'm innocent, I tell you! It's a trick. Someone planted the cosh and the wallet in my pockets while I was asleep... I've never seen them before.

What else can we do Tintin? The evidence is all against you.

I agree.

It's true. Everything points to my guilt. And the guard can swear I was trying to get away. Very neatly planned. But why? And by whom?

The key to the handcuffs! Well done, Snowy. Bring it here!

ZZZZ

ZZZ

Good gracious, we've stopped ..Good heavens, where's Tintin?

I...er...don't know.

He's given us the slip. Got away, with hand-cuffs, too. What a cheek! ...

To be precise: he's given us away. Slipped us the hand-cuffs, too. What a sneak! ...

An hour later...

Good! A village. Perhaps I can hire a car to take me to the coast.

CLINK
CLINK
CLINK

Just wait till I get my hands on him!

To be precise:...er ...just wait till we get our hands!

Hello!

Tintin!

!

You!

Hey, stop!

That's what they call putting your head in the lion's mouth!

Stop him! Stop him!

Where's he gone?

Excuse me, sir. Have you seen a young man running past your house?

Let me see. A young man, you say. That'd be him I saw, with a little white dog. Going like the wind, he was. Hid himself among those trees, over there.

Aha! We've got him!

Snowy!

WOOAH
WOOAH

!

Snowy's given the game away!

It's Tintin!

Stop! You're under arrest!

We're gaining on him!

To be precise: we're...

It's your own fault. If you'd kept quiet, none of this would have happened.

Here comes a lorry, going our way. I'll try to thumb a ride.

Lucky for me you're going right to the docks. I'm trying to catch the cross-channel ferry. Think we'll make it?

All right! Haul off the gangway!

So, my friend, we are safely away. Our little plan was a good one, eh?

Not bad at all! By the time Tintin has finished proving his innocence we shall be well clear...

WHEW!

Don't let him see us. We can't do anything here on the boat.

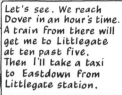
Let's see. We reach Dover in an hour's time. A train from there will get me to Littlegate at ten past five. Then I'll take a taxi to Eastdown from Littlegate station.

LITTLEGATE

WAY OUT

Can you drive me to Eastdown?

Yes, sir.

I'm glad to see you, Ivan...No time to explain. Follow that taxi.

Right!

Did you notice that car, Snowy... how it shot past us?

?

It's O.K., they're coming this way .. Ready?

Going to be long, mate?

I... don't know ... It's the brakes ... Something wrong...

!?

Fine!

Too easy!

Look, Puschov; our friend Tintin is coming round.

Aha!

So, you managed to escape from the police. It would have been wiser to stay safely behind bars.

Stop, Ivan. This will do.

O.K.

Get out! And don't try to be clever with me!

Don't you think this joke has gone far enough? What do you want with me?

You needn't put on an act for us. You know as well as we do.

Undo the rope.

Good. Now, my brilliant friend, you are going to become the world high-diving champion. Jump!

They're going to murder Tintin! Help! What can I do?

Go on, jump!

To make it look like an accident, I suppose?

Be-e-e-e

GRR

GNAAA

Get on with it... Jump! I'll count three... One!...

Two!? ❓

⚡ Good old Snowy!

All right... Hands up!

Look out! They're coming back!

?

Let's get out of here!

Don't worry, we'll make sure of him next time.

Come on, Snowy, we must get moving.

You have some brilliant ideas, Snowy. But don't let them run away with you!

Hello... Ja... Doctor Müller speaking... So, it is you... What?... Tintin on our trail... Kruzitürcken! We shall have to keep our eyes open.

Hello, the wreckage of the plane that crashed last night. Come on, let's have a look.

What a mess. What happened to the pilot?

Don't know, sir. We found this lot this morning. No sign of the crew. They must have baled out when they ran into trouble.

It's the plane I saw yesterday. Definitely. But I shan't learn much from this pile of scrap-metal.

Snowy!

Snowy's on to something!

He's picked up a scent; it must be the crew.

There isn't a dog in the world like him. He can smell out a crook a mile away.

Better be on our guard; we must be getting close.

Careful...Mustn't take any risks.

Here we go! He's found something.

★!?☄+★ ⚡⚡...!

Aren't you ashamed, wasting our time bone-hunting. Here, give it to me.

I've told you dozens of times, you're not to chew filthy old bones.

Here, Snowy! Come here at once!

WOOAH

WOOAH! WOOAH!

!?

Strange...He really does want me to follow him.

I'll come. But woe betide you if it's just another bone.

?

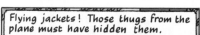
Flying jackets! Those thugs from the plane must have hidden them.

Too much to hope they'd leave anything in the pockets.

Aha! Look there! Some scraps of paper. Something's been torn up. Perhaps this will give us a lead.

I've always liked puzzles, and this time I've got a real one!

That's done it.

Eastdown
Sussex
Müller
3f t.

24 - 1 h.

Hmm. Not much help. What on earth can it mean? ...

Oh, Snowy, not again!

...and let that be an end of bones for today!

OUCH!

?

Can't you look what you're doing? ...Anyway, you're trespassing; this is private property.

I'm sorry. I didn't know. I lost my way...

All right, this time. But don't let me catch you again. Take the path down to the river, cross the bridge, and you'll see the main road.

Snowy! Are you trying to make a fool of me?

There's the road.

It must be a couple of miles to Eastdown.

?

Dr J.W. MÜLLER

No one about. I'll take a look around.

!

WOOF WOOF

WOOF! WOOF!

I'm done for!

WOOF! WOOF!

WOOF!! WOOF!!

WOOF!! WOOF!!

?

Snowy! Snowy! He'll be eaten alive!

WOOOF!

WOO-OO-OAH!

GRRR

Here, Snowy! Come here!

We must get out. The dog may have raised the alarm.

YEOW!

A man-trap!

RRRING

Ach so! Someone is caught in trap number nine. Let us take a look.

What a pleasant surprise! Tintin himself, come specially to see me.

Release him, Ivan. He won't run.

Get the car out. We're leaving at once.

It was a mistake to meddle in our affairs. I shall now have to dispose of you. Fortunately, I happen to be medical superintendent of a private mental institution: rather a special institution. Not all of my patients are insane when they are admitted...

...but after eight hours of ... special treatment, they are unlikely to recover. Excuse me: I must make a telephone call then I shall be entirely at your service.

I wonder...

Hello, Horncliffe?... I have a young patient for you... highly...er... dangerous. He will require treatment B... You understand? Good!

...a burning log?

Got one... hold it against the rope...

As usual, he seems entirely sane, but ...after the treatment...you follow me?

There!

And there!

?!

BANG

BANG

?!

BANG

BANG

Quick, my automatic!

CRACK

Kruzitürcken! It's empty!

CRASH

OW!

YEOW!

Ivan's gun... and it's still loaded!

Ach, I have him now!

THUD

BANG - BANG

ZZINGG

CHLOROFORM

FIRE! FIRE!

?

FIRE! FIRE!

Himmel! That burning log I threw: it set the room alight!

Fire? Is it a real alarm, or just a trick to make me open the door?

What's the matter? I feel dead tired...Come on, this is no time to fall asleep... I simply must ...

Look there!... A fire!

That's Dr Müller's place burning!

WHUⓊⓊⓊ UU

WHUⓊⓊⓊ UU

FIRE STATION

Fire crew ready for duty!

Good!

Come on, where's the key?

I must have put it somewhere...

Whatever shall we do? There's a hole in my pocket. The key must have fallen through as I ran...

Idiot! Come on, hurry! We'll have to search...

There it is!... Just in time; that magpie's got his eye on it!

?

Stop! Thief! Drop that key!

Got it!

AAH!

AAAH!

Open the door, quick!

All right... just a minute... I...

Goodness grac-ious! I've mixed them up This isn't the key to the station!

So there you are, Fred. How many times have I told you, that's the key to my jam cupboard!

DING DING DING

FIRE BRIGADE

What accursed luck! The fire brigade!

Anyone left inside the house, Doctor?

Fortunately not. We all escaped.

Wooah! Wooah! They must save Tintin! How can I make them understand? Wooah!

I must stop them at all costs, or they'll find him!

They're busy... now for it... no-one will notice me.

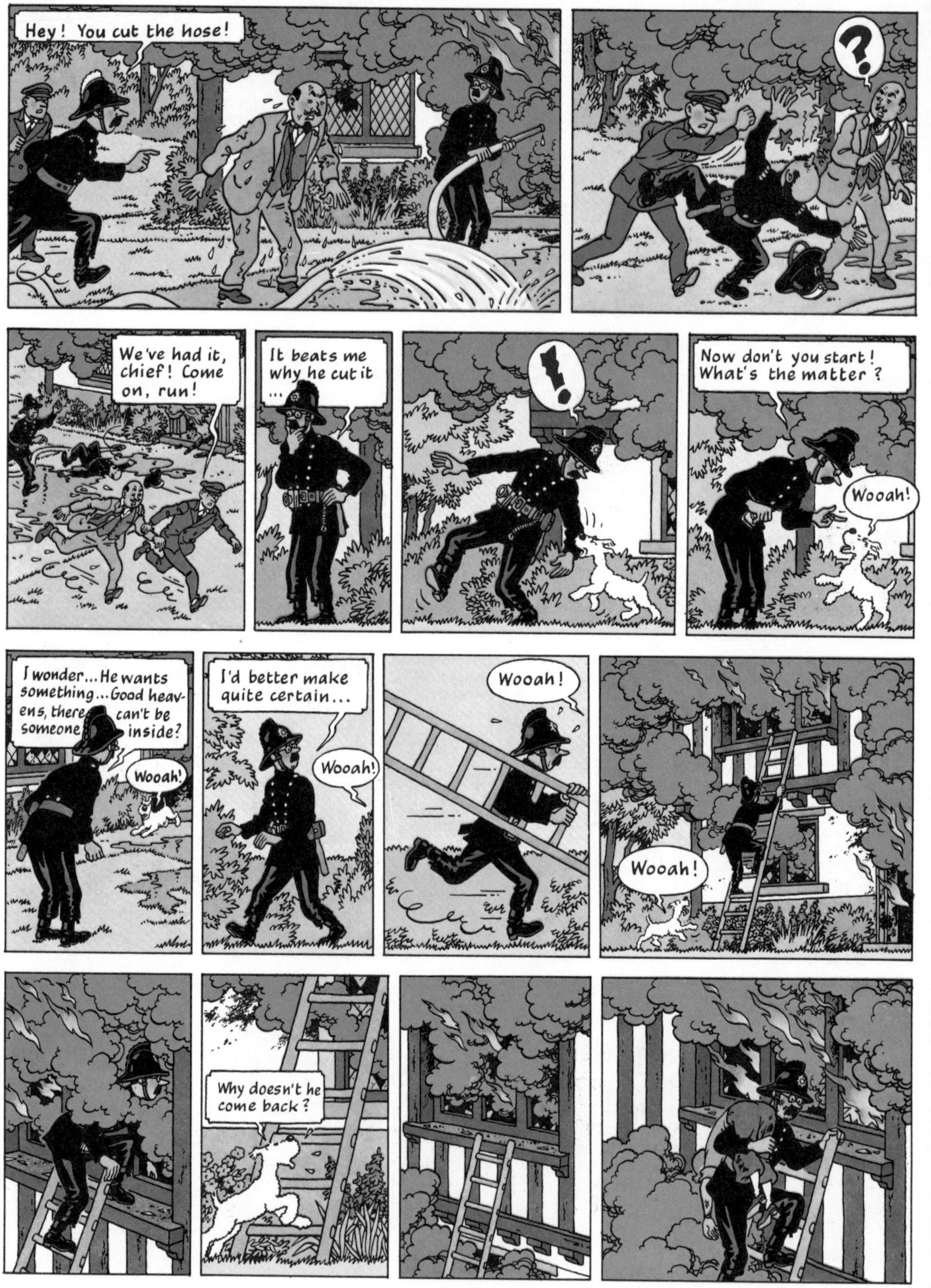

Hey! You cut the hose!
?
We've had it, chief! Come on, run!
It beats me why he cut it ...
!
Now don't you start! What's the matter?
Wooah!
I wonder... He wants something... Good heavens, there can't be someone inside?
Wooah!
I'd better make quite certain...
Wooah!
Wooah!
Wooah!
Why doesn't he come back?

Next morning...

...And what happened to Doctor Müller?

I'm afraid my men couldn't catch him. His car was standing just by the house. He hopped in, with his driver, and they went off at top speed. We hadn't a chance.

A pity. I'd give a lot to know ... why were they so anxious to get rid of me? Never mind Perhaps I'll find a clue at the house, to put me on their track again... The fire can't have destroyed everything ...

You're not getting out of bed?

Of course. I feel absolutely all right.

Heavens! There isn't much left of Dr. Müller's house: it's gutted.

I shan't find anything useful here...

?

Electric cables. What can they be for?

They seem to go on ...

How odd. Where on earth can they lead?

?

CRACK

?

A red beacon. I don't understand...

That isn't all. The wires continue along here.

I say, Tintin, are you going to do this all day?

There's another light here, too.

And now a third one...

The three trees are connected in a triangle...

GOT IT!

Müller
3 f. t.
24 1h.

These are instructions to the pilot in that plane. 3 f. r. △ means three flares, red, in a triangle. A signal!

Meanwhile...

And the worst of it is, another plane is due to deliver tonight. If the lights are not on he will go back without dropping his load. And I am running short of money...

We must return, Ivan. This is the plan. We enter the grounds after dark and light the beacons; the plane drops its load, which we put into the car. By tomorrow morning we can be out of the country. What do you think?

Good idea, chief.

That night...

Himmel! The cables have been pulled up. Someone has discovered our installation.

Look over there, chief. The beacons are alight!

Someone else is waiting for the plane! ... If they drop the load now we are finished! ... We have got to stop them. We must put out those lights. Here, help me to cut the wires.

But...but chief...the lights are still burning!

I wonder if they'll come tonight.

RRRRRR

?

O.K. to drop. I can see the lights.

Too late! There is the plane.

One out!

Great snakes-they've dropped something!

Let's see!

Tintin, confound him!

Two away!

THUMP

Another!

That fell quite close. It should be easier to spot than the first one.

I wonder what I'm going to find!

Last one!

Ivan!

Stop!

Stop!... Stop, or I'll fire!

He must think I'm daft!... He hasn't a hope of hitting me in the dark.

I'm warning you!

BANG

!?

Don't shoot!... I give in... I don't want to die!

?

Can I put my hands down now? I won't play any tricks.

Wake up, Tintin!

OHO!

Stupid fool! He trod on the rake and knocked himself out. I'll just take his gun...

Golly, what can I do?

WHAM

Quits!

Out cold!

The most important thing is to truss them up securely!

Necessity is the mother of invention, so they say. If you haven't any rope, use wire...

Now for the sacks. Let's see what they contain...

Great snakes! Banknotes!

Forgers! So that's your game. You'll go to gaol for this!

I'd better set about finding the other two sacks.

There's one...

?

EEK!
OWW!

They're getting away!

I'm an idiot! When they struggled, they caused a short-circuit, and the wires burned.

Hurry!

The car! They're getting away. Not a hope of stopping them... Unless...

It's my only chance ... If they come this way, it's still possible ...

He'll break his neck!

Aha! ...

Steady now... I must time it precisely ...

Whoops!

Why couldn't he use the gate, like me?... He always enjoys pretending to be an acrobat... Some people never learn!

94

To let them get away like that - right under my very nose!

Under his nose! They very nearly went over it!

A car! I'll stop it!

PARP
PAARP

There's a car just ahead... crooks making a getaway... I simply must go after them...

Crooks?... I say, what a lark!... Hop in the caravan.

We aren't exactly beating the land-speed record! We'll catch them... provided they have a puncture!

The old girl's a bit sluggish; we'll be O.K.when she warms up.

Didn't I say so?... Better already!

Now we're for it!

SPLOSH

Now then, I'm booking you for camping on private property... And in the second place, you've been picking unauthorised fruit... And the third offence, swimming in a manner liable to cause a breach of the peace!

NO BATHING

95

Oh well, there's no hope of catching them now.

Look, a smash.

Great snakes! It's their car!... Will you drop me here, please?

The occupants?... Not a scratch. I saw them go off towards the railway station...

They're going to catch that train!

♪

The train's pulling out!

?

He'll go flat on his face again! Just watch!

Come on, Snowy!

I made it - this time!

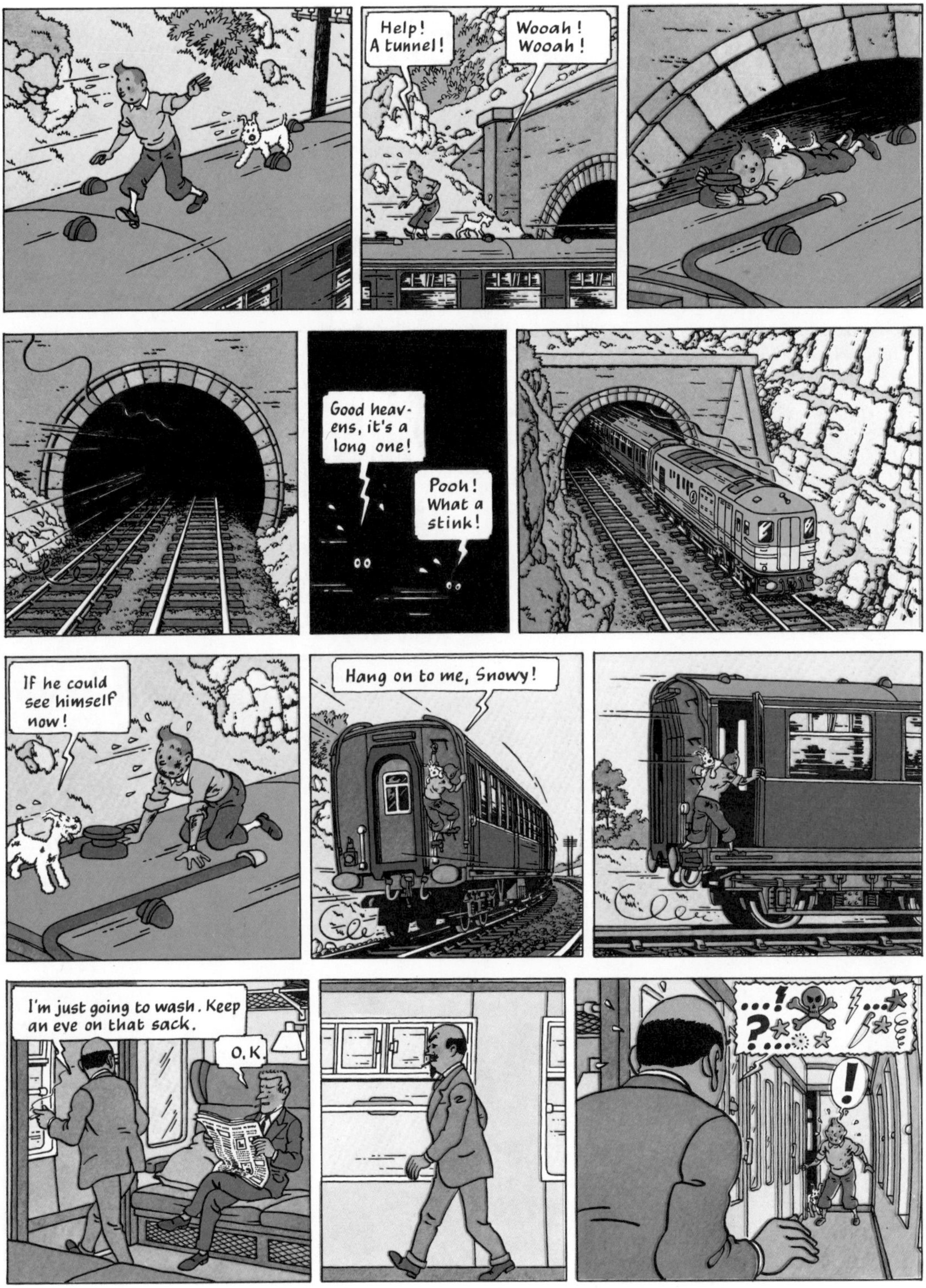
Help! A tunnel!
Wooah! Wooah!
Good heavens, it's a long one!
Pooh! What a stink!
If he could see himself now!
Hang on to me, Snowy!
I'm just going to wash. Keep an eye on that sack.
O.K.
...!
!

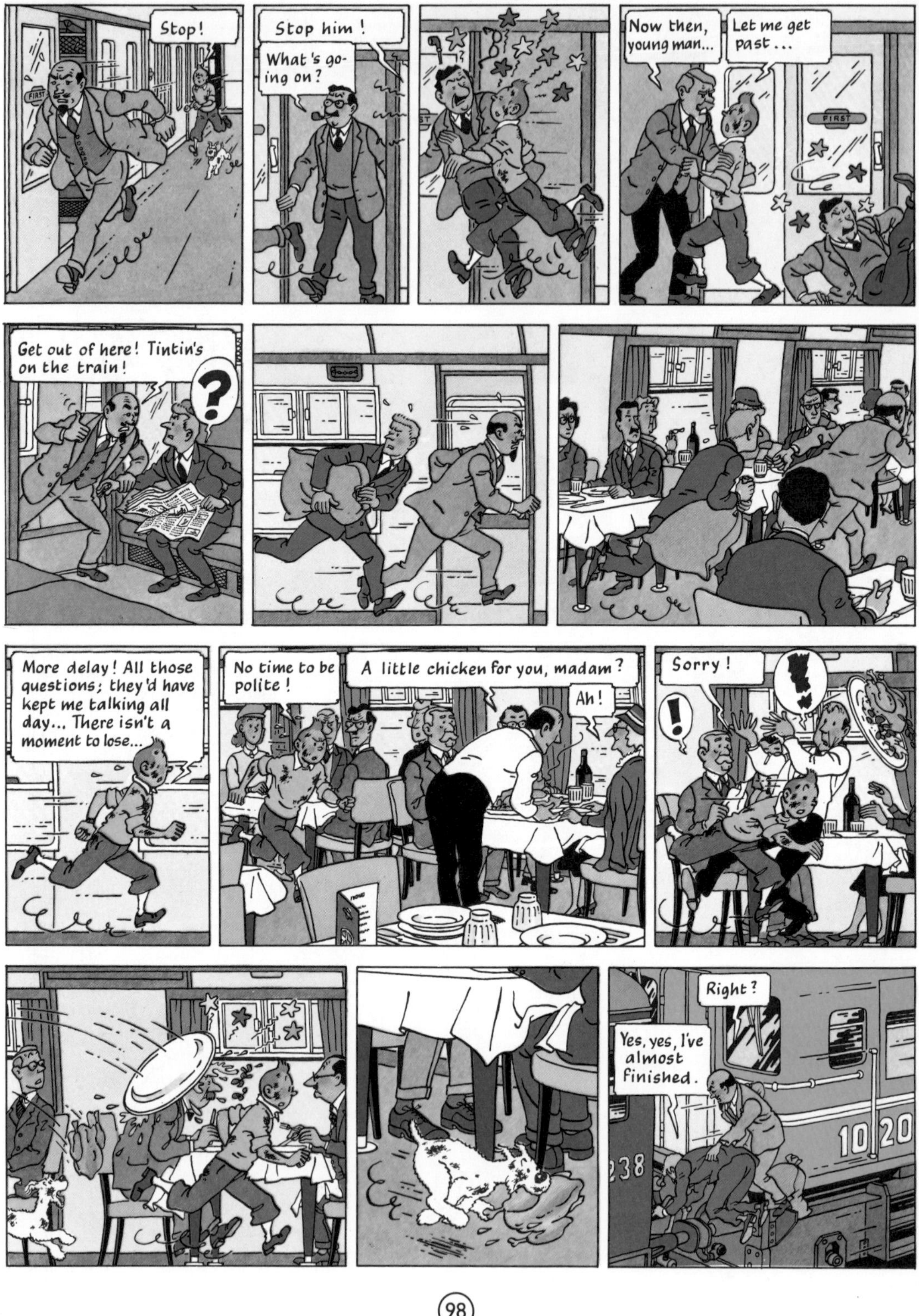
Stop!
Stop him!
What's going on?
Now then, young man...
Let me get past...
Get out of here! Tintin's on the train!
?
More delay! All those questions; they'd have kept me talking all day... There isn't a moment to lose...
No time to be polite!
A little chicken for you, madam?
Ah!
Sorry!
!
Right?
Yes, yes, I've almost finished.

Hey, what's going on? The train's pulling up.

That's it. The automatic brake will soon stop the coaches.

Bravo!

They've got away... cunning devils!

Can't say I'm sorry. Now I can enjoy my dinner in peace.

Come on, Snowy, we've no time to hang around. It may be hours before a relief engine arrives.

Look, Snowy, we're in luck! There's a goods train just moving off.

Hup!

LOCH LOMON WHISKY

Oops!

Long time since this was an egg!

LOCH LOMOND WHISKY

Hello, it's raining.

Golly, that's not water! But it's got a certain something, all the same!

Aha! There must be a leak...

Better try to clean myself up.

STOP!

A station?... No... Then I wonder why they've stopped.

What in the world...? An engine, just sitting there..

It's the one they hijacked. Müller must have abandoned it... But where did they go? The driver may give me a lead ...

Bert! Are you all right? What happened?

A couple of thugs... climbed into the cab... made us drive on ... then ordered me to stop. One of 'em got behind us, clobbered me with a spanner... I went out like a light. Didn't see which way they went ...

That's all right. My dog will pick up their trail in a flash... Snowy!

Now where's he gone?... Snowy!... Hey, Snowy!

SNOWY!

S'O.K., I'm c-c-coming...Give... hic... give a dog a sh-sh-shance...

Good heavens, he's tight!

Jush...hic... jush look what I can ... do!

You ought to be ashamed of yourself!... Disgusting!...You're worse than a mongrel from the gutter!

Now pull yourself together, and pick up the scent. We're chasing gangsters...remember?

It's not...hic...fair ...Hic...Two of you ...picking on a ...hic... poor little dog!...

Ah, a pub...and Snowy's got wind of something!

Wooah!

He's after them! He never really lets me down.

Wooah!

YE WHITE HART

Wooah! Wooah!

!?★ !

LOCH LOMOND WHISKY

If you don't watch out you'll come to a sticky end!

LOMOND ISKY

?

Himmel!

?

So we meet again, eh?

⁉

Great snakes!

What?

You won't get away this time!

Whoa there! Not so fast!

Let me go!... Don't you understand?...They're thugs, gangsters...They'll escape!

We know your little tricks!

How did he manage to get here so soon?

WHITE HART

It's absurd...they're crooks, I tell you...and you're letting them get away.

So you say. In the meantime we're arresting you...The robbery on the train: or have you forgotten that little episode?

It's ridiculous! You're not still flogging that dead horse?... Look here, let's make a deal. Don't arrest me till those thugs are behind bars, then I'll give myself up.

Hmm!... What do you think?

Hmm!... It's...er...highly irregular... But on second thoughts, we might...er...stretch a point.

All right, we agree. We'll let you go, on one condition: we come with you.

Two minds with one thought, eh? If he pulls something off, we get all the credit.

Keep it up, Snowy!

I only hope we're not too late!

HALCHESTER FLYING CLUB

PARKING

Look! Over there! That plane taking off... I bet it's them!

Watch out! He's diving at us!

G-AREI

Ruffians!

To be precise: road-hogs!

G-AREI

Our hats...?

There.

The vandals! Our best hats, almost brand new...a pair of perfect bowlers!

I remember when we bought them, seven years ago...A bowl of perfect purlers!

I'm beginning to agree with Tintin: they look like crooks.

To be precise: so do I. Tintin may be right: they cook like rooks!

RRR

? ?

Wait for me, I'll be back! Goodbye!

Come on! After them! That other machine over there... Quick!

We're police officers... Start her up... We're taking off right away!

But sir, I...

That's enough! No ifs or buts! We're the police, see? And we're commandeering this plane, and you to fly it!

Police... Understand?

Full throttle, pilot!

You can cut out the... er... aerobatics!

I'm s-s-sorry, s-s-sir... I'm d-d-doing my b-best... It's the f-f-first time I've f-f-flown... I'm just the m-m-mechanic!

We'll soon be on their tail, unless...

Just as I feared... Running into cloud...

Rotten visibility... We've lost sight of them.

Have to land... We're near the coast... don't want to drop in the drink.

Doesn't look too rough. I'll have a go...

A wall! We're done for!

CRASH
CRACK
?

You all right? Och, the puir wee laddie! He's fallen inta the brambles.

Come ben the hoose. I'll gi'e ye some mair clothes. It's nae far.

A neer thing...
That's putting it mildly!

Listen, that's the sound of a plane. You won't be able to see it in this mist.

We positively insist. Put us down!
But I keep on telling you: I don't know how to land.

The controls, you idiot! Don't take your hands off the wheel!

Whew! I thought my last hour had come.
To be precise: mine too!

In ye go.

Ye'll find a'ye need i' the other room.
Thanks.
?

A'richt?
Fine! I'm coming down.

There!

OH!

Snowy! Up to your old tricks again!

LOCH LOMOND WHISKY

That certainly seems to be the best solution...

...And let this be a lesson, you drunken, disobedient dog!

Our friend has suggested that we spend the night here. It's getting late.

That's an invitation we'll certainly accept. How very kind of you.

Next morning...

...The dense fog that blanketed the British Isles during the night caused a number of accidents...

Off the Scottish coast this morning, fishermen from Kiltoch discovered floating wreckage of a light aircraft registration G-AREI. There was no trace of the crew, who are presumed drowned.

G-AREI!... The plane we followed: the same registration...Well, that puts paid to that. They're dead, poor devils.

Maybe, but I'd like to be absolutely sure. I'm going to Kiltoch to look around.

It's no above fifteen miles tae Kiltoch. But mind ye keep tae the path thra' the glen.

Thanks!

Fifteen miles: that's quite a step. We shan't get to Kiltoch before evening.

!?

Snowy! Come here!

Wooah!

Wooah! Wooah!

WOOAAH!

WOOAH! ?

WOOAH!

My poor Snowy!

Whatever made you sit on a thistle?

I can smell the sea. We must be fairly close, now.

Look, there's Kiltoch!

'Evening.

I wonder if you could put me up for the night?

Aye, for sure.

That's fine. I'd like something to eat, too, please... I've just arrived in Kiltoch... and heard about the air crash. Poor fellows. Do you know, have they recovered the bodies?

No, there's no even a sign o' them yet.

And no more there wull be, neether. ? ?

Nivver! Why not?...

Why not, ye say?...Ha! Ha! Ha! A'body can see you're no frae these parts, laddie, else ye'd ken for why they'll no be seen agen. Have ye no haird tell o' THE BEAST?

The beast? ... What beast? ... The Loch Ness Monster? | Haud yer whisht, laddie, A'm speirin' o' the beast that bides on the Black Island, i' the ruins o' the castle o' Craig Dhui. The critter's for devourin' ev'ry maun that's sae bold as to gang neer the place. | I mind...it'll be three months back, twa young laddies were for explorin' the island, for a' our wurds o' warnin'. They went off in a wee boat. Dead calm it was: not a breath o' wund...And d'ye ken, they were nivver haird of agen!... And it'll be last yeer, a Kiltoch fisherman vanished wi'out a sign ... | A dreich mist there was that day...Puir MacGregor! 'Tis sure he ran aground on the island...and he's nae been seen sunce! And twa yeers back...och, but there's nae end to the tales o' them that's gone, puir sauls ...

Och! 'Tis a terrible beast!...There's times in the nicht, when the wund's frae the sea, ye can heer it... Whisht! D'ye heer?

THUMP THUMP
?

Here's your tea, sir.
Thanks. You know, it's odd about that crash. I think I'll visit the Black Island tomorrow.

The next morning ...

Will you take me across to the Black Island? | The Black Island? For why are ye wantin' ta gae to the Black Island? Are ye wearied o' livin'?

Whit's that? Tak ye tae the Black Island?... No for a' the bawbees i' the wurld! A'm no for deein' yet, laddie! | Tae the Black Island? Mind what I say, there's no maun heer that'll dare go neer that curst place. | Aha! Just what I'm looking for! | Ahoy there! Will you let me hire your boat? | Aye laddie, but d'ye ken work the outboard motor? ... | Wha' are ye makin' for this bra day?
Er... I want to have a look at the castle of Craig Dhui.

The Black Island? Nae fear! Ye'll no come back agen and ma boat'll be lost!
What if I buy your boat? | Off we go! | Anither awa' tae his doom ...

They were quite right in Kiltoch... It is a sinister place...

I think we'll explore the castle first.

That must be the staircase to the tower.

What a marvellous view!

THUMP THUMP

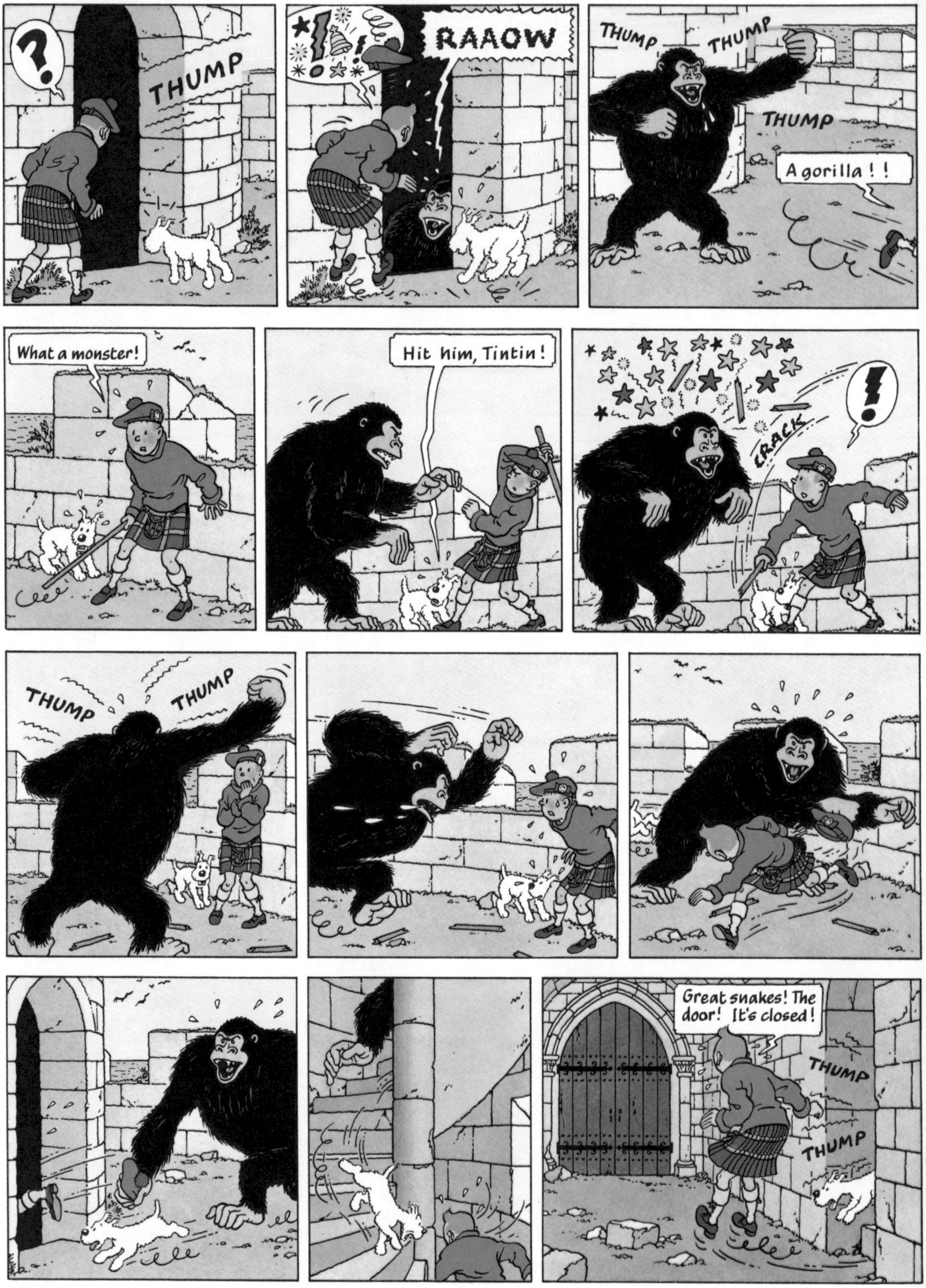
?
THUMP
RAAOW
THUMP
THUMP
THUMP
A gorilla ! !
What a monster!
Hit him, Tintin!
CRACK
!
THUMP
THUMP
Great snakes! The door! It's closed!
THUMP
THUMP

It's locked!... We're caught in a trap!

Come on, let's find another way out...

THUMP

Too late!

If I can't knock him out this time, we're finished!

RHAAH!

Don't miss, Tintin!

Good heavens! He didn't even feel it!

BONK

What's he doing? He seems to be looking for something...

Crumbs!

RHAAH! RHAAH!

CRASH

Saved!

Saved!

RHAAH!

WOOAH!

Run for dear life! Back to the boat!

It's vanished!

What do we do now, Snowy?

Go on! Seek them, Ranko! Seek them!

Seek them, Ranko, seek them!

The gorilla! There's a man with him, too.

RHAAH!

WOOAH!

A cave! Well done, Snowy! Perhaps I can squeeze in...

Wooah!

What a stroke of luck ... it widens out.

Ssh! They're coming...

Go on, Ranko!... Go on!

Aha! So that's where he's hiding. We've got him now!

RHAAH!

Help! He's smelt us out! Thank goodness the entrance is so narrow...

WOOAH

Congratulations, my dear Tintin, you've made a brilliant getaway ...You even managed to evade our faithful Ranko...You are quite safe in your cave... Except...

There's one enemy you won't escape: the sea, my dear Tintin. You have forgotten the sea. The tide is rising. Unless you prefer to come out and meet little Ranko again, you'll drown in your hole like a rat!

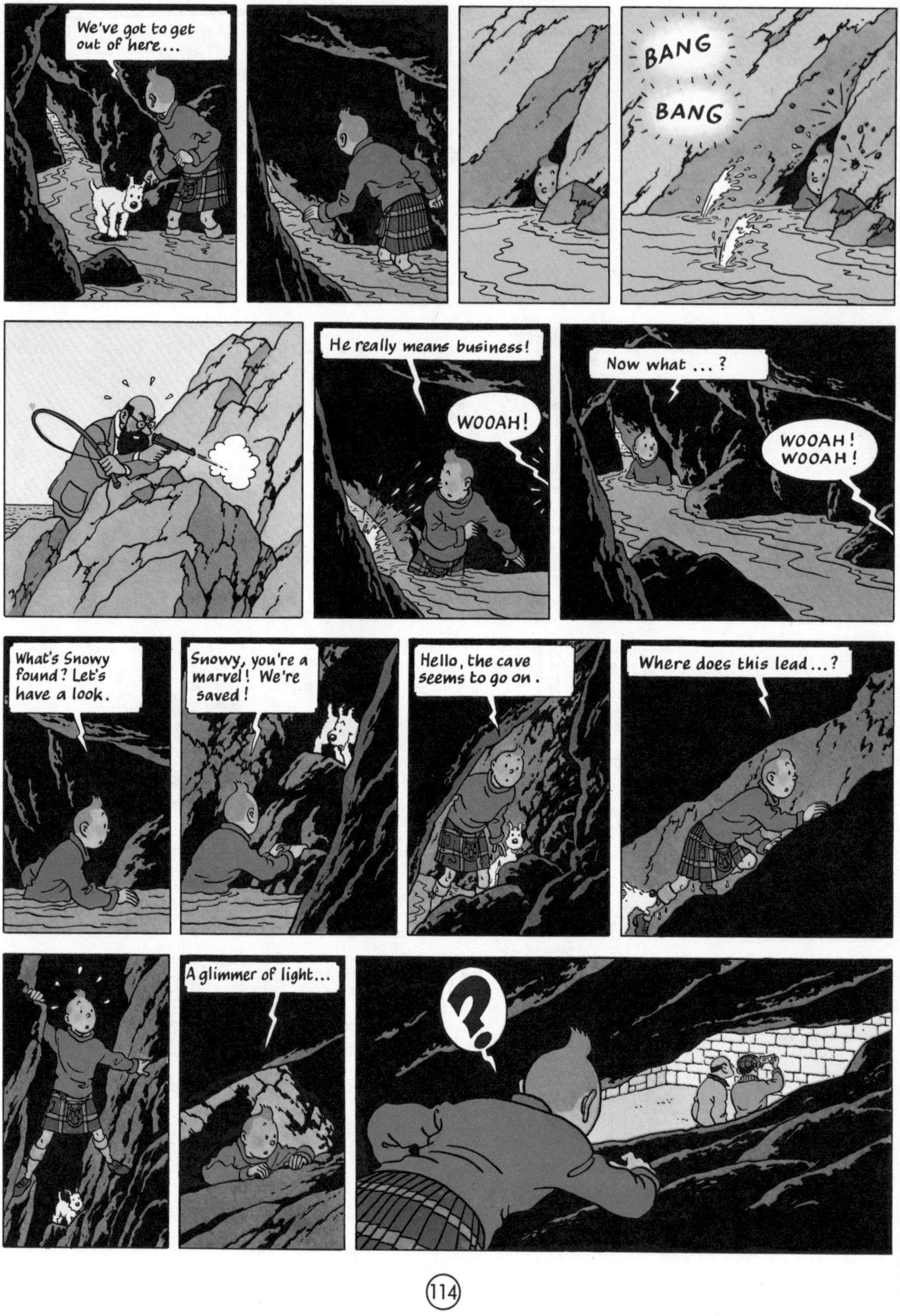

We've got to get out of here...
BANG
BANG
He really means business!
WOOAH!
Now what ...?
WOOAH! WOOAH!
What's Snowy found? Let's have a look.
Snowy, you're a marvel! We're saved!
Hello, the cave seems to go on.
Where does this lead...?
A glimmer of light...
?

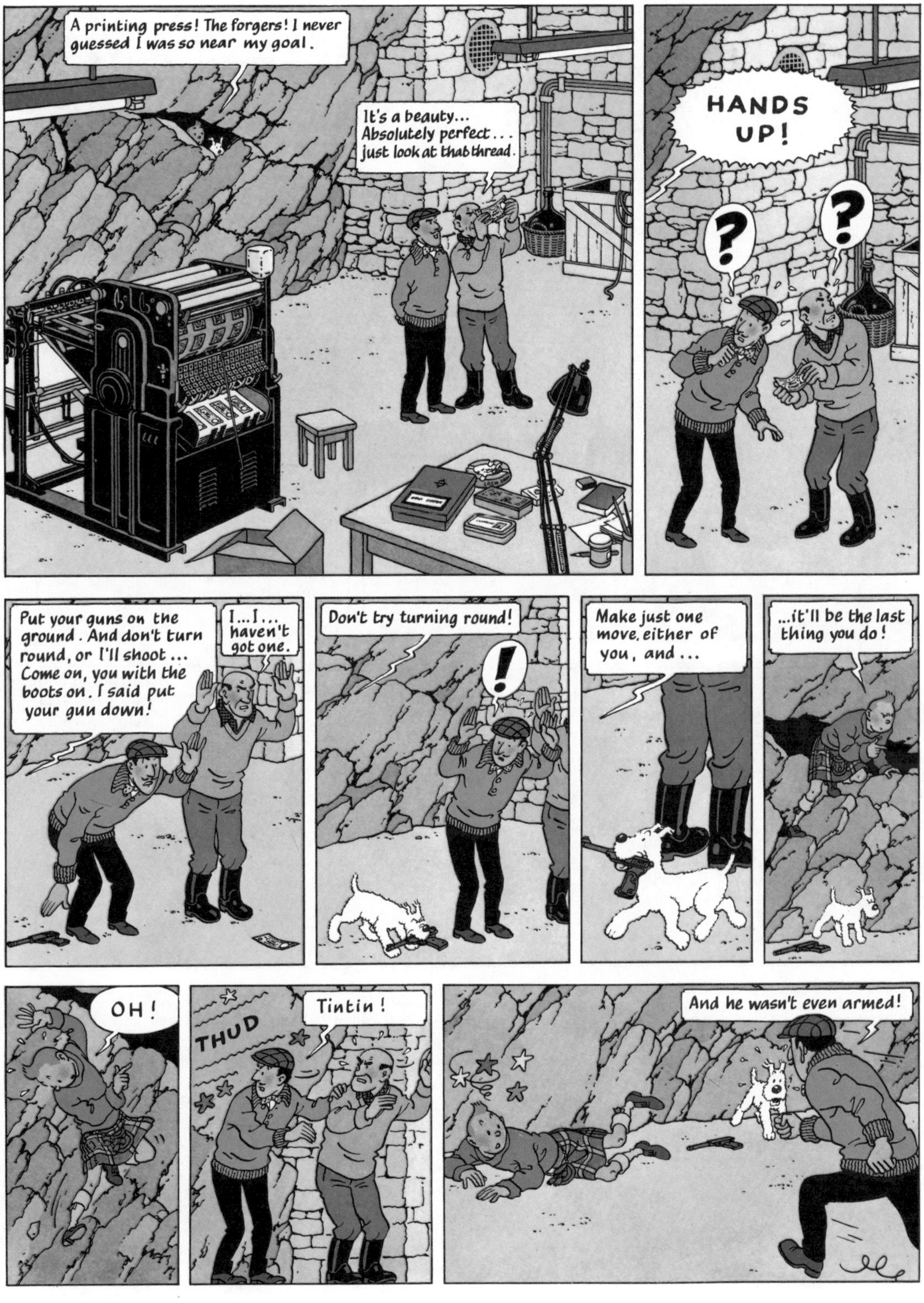
A printing press! The forgers! I never guessed I was so near my goal.
It's a beauty... Absolutely perfect... just look at thab thread.
HANDS UP!
?
?
Put your guns on the ground. And don't turn round, or I'll shoot... Come on, you with the boots on. I said put your gun down!
I...I... haven't got one.
Don't try turning round!
!
Make just one move, either of you, and...
...it'll be the last thing you do!
OH!
THUD
Tintin!
And he wasn't even armed!

Get back! And put up your hands!

That's enough horseplay. There's a coil of rope over there. You, puss-in-boots, bring it here and tie up your friend with the whiskers. And make a good job of it!

Get a move on! Pull that rope tight, as well. I don't want to have to shoot you.

Your turn now...There, that'll do... It's amazing how quickly thugs come to their senses at the wrong end of a loaded gun.

A loaded gun??... Of all the stupid clods!... I've just remembered: there's no ammunition in my pistol!

A fine time to think of that!

Great snakes! He's right. It's completely empty!

Help! Help!... Rescue!... Help! Help!

Help!... Help! Tintin's here...Help! Help!... Help!

Stop that! Shut up, or I'll...

Go ahead...threaten us! Words won't keep us quiet... Aren't you forgetting that gun isn't loaded?

Maybe. But there's more than one way of using an automatic....I'll demonstrate!

Golly, that's the stuff, Tintin!...One!... Two!..Knockout!

Too late! They've raised the alarm... I can hear footsteps... someone coming...

Quick! An ink roller...One of those will be more effective than an empty gun.

No one here!

We're too late, he's gone.

This is Tintin's handiwork, and no mistake! The schweinhund made off when he heard us coming. Go and warn the boss... And hurry!

My old friends ...Dr Müller ... and his man Ivan!

Ivan!... I ...

THUD

What is it, chief?

Any more?... Doesn't look like it... Good! That gives me a chance to take care of this lot!

There, that'll do. And be good boys while I'm away!

WOOAAH

Fully loaded: that's better. Still, I hope I shan't need to use it... Now, let's go...

O.K. But mind what you're doing this time!

A good day's work, Ranko!...That's disposed of Tintin, once and for all.

Then let me be the first to congratulate you!

A ghost! Tintin's ghost!

Spirit of the dead! Have mercy on me!... Mercy!

He's gone off his head!

Spare me!... For pity's sake, forgive me... forgive me!

YEOW!

That's a little jujitsu, my clever friend!

And that's a straight left to the jaw!

RRAAH!

Let's see what effect this will have...

BANG

OH!

He'll eat Tintin!

WOOAH!

**WOOAH!
WOOAH!
WOOAH!**

That's got rid of him!
Now to help Tintin.

Golly, what's the
matter now?

Oh, it's only him
again...Watch this!

WOOAH!

You frighten him to death, Snowy!

Silly, isn't it?...
Imagine, a great
big animal like
that scared out of
his wits by a tiny
little...

Snowy!...Snowy!... Where are you, Snowy?

Ah, there you are, lionheart! ...Come on, we've got to search the rest of this place.

Lionheart! ...Very funny!

Sh! I can hear some-one talking... on the other side of that door.

He's won the first round, but let's see what happens now...He could make a mistake...This is it, he's coming towards us...

Hands up!

It's only a tele-vision set!

One final loop...

...and Johnny James, aero-batic champion, comes in to land...Just listen to the crowd cheering!

Some sort of air dis- play.

The next item in our telerecording, high speed formation flying by a squadron from R.A.F. Fighter Command.

Let's have a look at that desk...

Good heavens! What a stroke of luck: a list of all their con-tacts!... Czechoslovakia, Ger-many, France, Holland, Austria, ...All over the place... What a catch for the police!

- 3 -

- Hansa Släsxeck - Praha
  Sdrodjz, 45

- Otto Steinkopf
  Hedemanstrasse, 18 Potsdam

- Louis Bonvault
  Villa Gai-Soleil
  St Germain (S.et O.)

Kees Nieuwenhuis
Zilverdijk, 73 Amsterdam

Werner Schelhammer
...Wien

And here comes another com-petitor...Number...number...Hello, he doesn't seem to be listed on the official programme...But what does that matter?...He's really terrific! Just look at that!...He must have nerves of steel!

This is incredible...He's a genius ...pilots his plane with superb confidence...a fantastic series of aerobatics...

LAND! In the name of the law!

I... I only wish I could!

Now the plane comes roaring down, skims over the field and shoots up like a rocket ...

Stop! We want to get down, d'you hear?

G-AIRJ

Now he's heading for the ground again...and into another flawless loop he goes, then...Good heavens! one of the passengers has slipped out of his seat...This is terrible!

G-AIRJ

G-AIRJ

G-

Whew! What a stunt! That really had us fooled!

And this time he really is coming down... He's going to land... He's cut the motor...

He touches down... the plane bounces ...

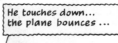

...and does one last, hair-raising somersault before it comes to rest in the centre of the field.

A clear victory! The judges are unanimous ...the aerobatic championship is yours!

I mustn't waste time... Let's see what else they've got...

A radio transmitter! I'm in luck!

SOS...SOS...Calling the police... Calling the police...This is an emergency... Are you receiving me?...

Police control... Police control...We are receiving you loud and clear ...Come in please.

It's that secret transmitter... The one we've been hunting for the past three months...

They can hear me!

Tintin calling the police...Tintin calling... I'm on the Black Island, off Kiltoch. I've rounded up a gang of forgers and am holding them here. Can you send a squad to pick them up?...Over!

Police control... Police control... Message received and understood. We will send help at once. Good luck, Tintin!...We'll keep in touch with you... Over and out!

Well, that's that! The police will be here soon, then we'll be able to say goodbye to the Black Island.

About time too. I've had enough of this mediaeval menagerie!

Crumbs! He's managed to free himself!

Now we're for it!...The others will all be loose, as well; we shall have the whole gang after us!

Quietly...Quietly...Here, load your guns. I don't want any mistakes this time!

Don't worry, we'll make him pay for what he did to us!

Sssh!

122

There!

You go round outside and cut off his retreat.

ZZZING

Got you!

Trapped!

BANG

BANG

He's taken refuge in the tower.

Excellent! We've got him cornered!

Police control... Police control calling Tintin... We are coming to your assistance... A police launch is heading for the Black Island at full speed. Two detectives are with the officers on board... End of message. Over to you... Tintin... Tintin are you receiving me?... Come in, please...

Crumbs! No more ammunition!... I'm done for!

Come on! His gun's empty. Bring him down!

123

Thank goodness I've still got something...

There's the Black Island. Only a few minutes and we'll be ashore.

I'm going to fetch Ranko. At least he won't be put off by a few stones...

That seems to have cooled their enthusiasm...

RRR
RRRZ
I can hear an engine...

Hooray!... The police!

RRRAH!

WOOAH

Ranko won't be long!

Ready... Steady...

Wait for me!　Go!

?

If you'd done as I said ...

Mind the bump! ...

Drop your guns!　The police! We've had it!

Tintin! You can come out now. It's all right...　It's us!

Come on, Snowy, our troubles are over... Down we go!

I'm so sorry... I tripped over a stone...

Oh?

Really?

What happened? Did they put up much of a fight?

No, no... To quote Christopher Columbus... er... Captain Cook... er... well, someone about that time: "We came, we saw, we conquered!"

Splendid!... Before we go, I want to have a last look round. Why don't you come with me?

A plane!

But what about an airfield? How did they... er... land?

We shall see. There's a door over there, with a steel shutter.

The beach at low tide... You see? That was their airstrip.

Here's another lot of those sacks, full of forged notes ready for dispatch.

Brrr! It's cold down here. Let's go on up.

Between ourselves, I shan't be sorry to leave this place... I... er... Do you ...er... believe in ghosts?

Me?... Believe in ghosts? Ha! Ha! H...

WOO HOO HOOO °°

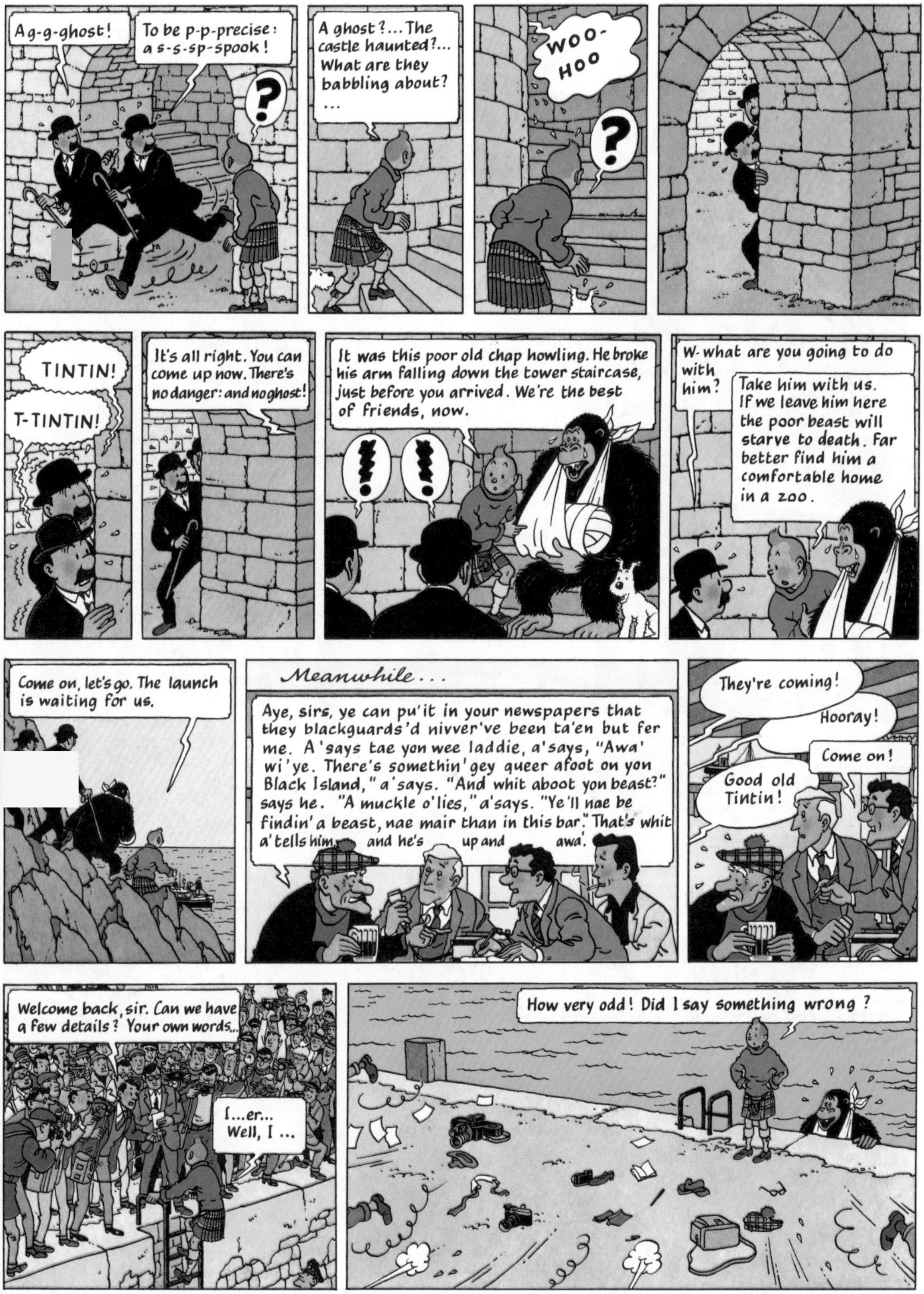
A g-g-ghost!
To be p-p-precise: a s-s-sp-spook!
?
A ghost?... The castle haunted?... What are they babbling about? ...
WOO-HOO
?
TINTIN!
T-TINTIN!
It's all right. You can come up now. There's no danger: and no ghost!
It was this poor old chap howling. He broke his arm falling down the tower staircase, just before you arrived. We're the best of friends, now.
W-what are you going to do with him?
Take him with us. If we leave him here the poor beast will starve to death. Far better find him a comfortable home in a zoo.
Come on, let's go. The launch is waiting for us.
Meanwhile . . .
Aye, sirs, ye can pu'it in your newspapers that they blackguards'd nivver've been ta'en but fer me. A'says tae yon wee laddie, a'says, "Awa' wi'ye. There's somethin' gey queer afoot on yon Black Island," a'says. "And whit aboot yon beast?" says he. "A muckle o'lies," a'says. "Ye'll nae be findin' a beast, nae mair than in this bar." That's whit a'tells him, and he's up and awa'.
They're coming!
Hooray!
Come on!
Good old Tintin!
Welcome back, sir. Can we have a few details? Your own words...
I...er... Well, I ...
How very odd! Did I say something wrong?

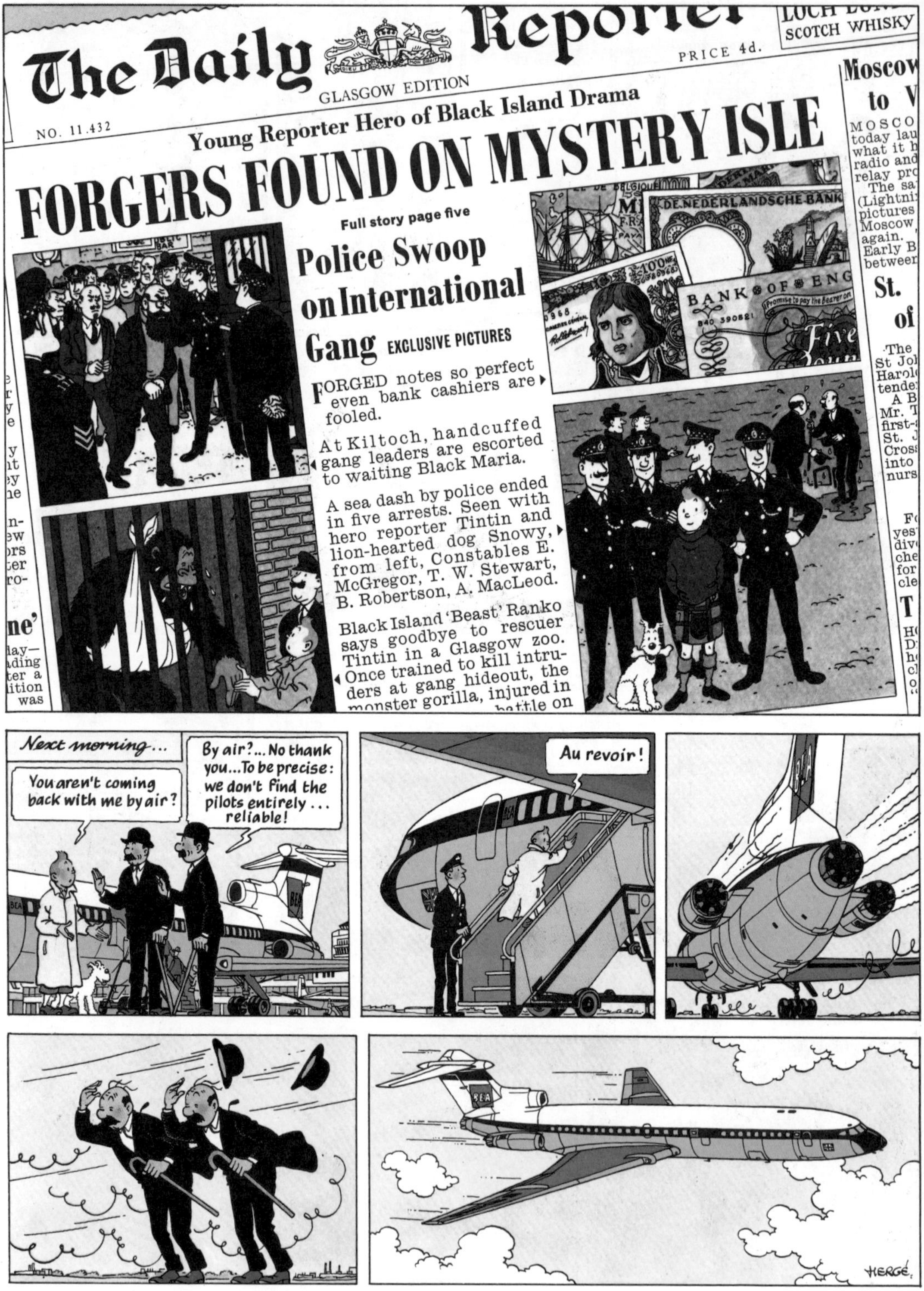
The Daily Reporter
SCOTCH WHISKY
PRICE 4d.
GLASGOW EDITION
NO. 11.432
Young Reporter Hero of Black Island Drama
FORGERS FOUND ON MYSTERY ISLE
Full story page five
Police Swoop on International Gang
EXCLUSIVE PICTURES
FORGED notes so perfect even bank cashiers are fooled.
At Kiltoch, handcuffed gang leaders are escorted to waiting Black Maria.
A sea dash by police ended in five arrests. Seen with hero reporter Tintin and lion-hearted dog Snowy, from left, Constables E. McGregor, T. W. Stewart, B. Robertson, A. MacLeod.
Black Island 'Beast' Ranko says goodbye to rescuer Tintin in a Glasgow zoo. Once trained to kill intruders at gang hideout, the monster gorilla, injured in
DE NEDERLANDSCHE BANK
BANK OF ENG
Promise to pay the Bearer on
Moscow
to V
MOSCO
today lau
what it h
radio and
relay pro
Next morning...
You aren't coming back with me by air?
By air?... No thank you... To be precise: we don't find the pilots entirely ... reliable!
Au revoir!
BEA
HERGÉ

HERGÉ
THE ADVENTURES OF TINTIN

KING OTTOKAR'S SCEPTRE

eih bennek · eih blåvek

King Ottokar's Sceptre

KING OTTOKAR'S SCEPTRE

Let's sit down on this bench for a minute.

Hello, someone has left his brief-case behind.

I can't see anybody...

Perhaps I ought to open it? The owner's name might be inside.

Here it is!... 'Hector Alembick, 24, Flyaway Road'.

That's not far. I'll take it back.

You're making a mistake, Tintin!... No good ever comes of getting mixed up in other people's business.

FLYAWAY ROAD

Professor Alembick? Third floor, first door on the right...

24

RAT TAT TAT

Come in!

Oh, good-evening, Mrs. Piggott. Put it all on the little table, will you?

It's not Mrs. Piggott, Professor. I've brought back your brief-case.

What?...

My brief-case?

Ssh! Someone's just come to see him...

How very kind of you to return it. I'm especially grateful, as the text of the paper I am reading to the I.S.A. Congress tonight is in there.

The I.S.A.?

I.S.A: International Sigillographical Association.

Sigi... what?

Sigillography. Do you mean you've never heard of it? It's the science concerned with the study of seals. It's extremely interesting and... A cigarette?.

No thank you: I don't smoke.

Yes, sigillography is an absorbing study. One look at my collection will convince you.

?

WOOAH

Oh, good gracious! I'm so sorry! I have a dreadful habit of dropping my cigarette ends about!

This is one of the rarest items in my collection: the seal of Charlemagne. Here is the seal of Edward the Confessor, and next to it one which belonged to Gradenigo, Doge of Venice. And here's another fine specimen: an intaglio ring from the Saxon period

...And this is a very unusual seal, which I found quite by chance in Prague. It is the seal of Ottokar IV, King of Syldavia...

Oh?..

It is one of the few seals we know of from that country. But there must be others, and I am going to Syldavia to study the problem on the spot.

The Syldavian Ambassador, an old friend of mine, has promised to give me letters of introduction. I hope I shall be allowed to go through the historic national archives. A cigarette?...

No, thank you... And when are you leaving?

As soon as I have found a secretary. At least, rather more than a secretary; I really need someone to take care of all the details of my journey, like hotels, passports, luggage and so on.

But I see that you have become interested in sigillography too. Let me have your name and address and I will send you my booklet: 'How to become a sigillographer.'

How very kind of you...

He's going... Quick, meet him on the stairs...

Steady!..Here he comes!

CLICK

That's a funny place to put a watch right...

Got it!... Wonderful, the way a miniature camera can be hidden in a watch...

Here!..

We'll develop the picture right away.

!?

Is it O.K.?

Bother! I've left my book at Professor Alembick's flat.

Anyway, we know his name is Tintin.

2nd FLOOR

Tintin!...Tintin!...You know that a name by itself won't do...We must have a photograph!

Well, I've had enough...I'm off... If anyone wants me, I'm at the 'KLOW'!... Goodbye!...

Goodbye!

24

This is all very mysterious... Let's follow him.

-KLOW-

SYLDAVIAN RESTAURANT

Well, well! 'Syldavian Restaurant'. The plot thickens!

Let's go in!

-KLOW-

SYLDAVIA

Hello?... Where's he gone?

A customer!...

Er... I'd like... something to eat... please...

Will you take a seat, sir?...

What would you like, sir?...

Er... bring me... er... a 'szlaszeck' with mushrooms ... and a glass of 'szpradj'...

But I'd like a wash first...

The cloakroom is at the end of the passage.

...As for Professor Alembick, we'll have to wait for a day or two, until he's got the papers from the Embassy...

Ahem!

!

At the end of the passage, sir ...

I'm sorry, I misunderstood.

Did he catch me listening at the door?

...and he was listening outside the door! He's a young chap with a funny tuft of hair... There's a dog with him.

I'll bet a thousand khors it's the fellow Sporovitch tried to photograph!...

Where's Snowy got to?...

TING
TING
TING

My bill, please...

In a moment, sir...

?

·KLOW·
SYLDAVIAN RESTAURANT
38, NIGHTINGALE ROAD
PROP: J. KNOSZVITCH

1 szlaszeck dany· 1·20
1 Szpäs   ·60
                1·80
Sunia 10%   ·18
                1·98

Danger awaits the one who dares
To poke his nose in others' affairs
- SYLDAVIAN PROVERB~

What does this mean?

What, sir?... Oh, yes... Don't you know the old Syldavian custom, sir?... In res- taurants in my country there 's always a proverb or a short motto on the bill.

Oh, really?

Yes, sir. Rather nice, isn't it?... Thank you, just right... I hope you enjoyed your meal, sir? ...

Very much, thank you. Your 'szlaszeck' was excellent. How do you make it?

Ah, it's one of our specialities: the hind leg of a young dog, in Syldavian sauce...

SNOWY!

SNOWY!
SNOWY!

?

Ah, there you are! ...Where have you been hiding?

I hope you will come again, sir.

Ha! ha! ha! We shan't see him again in a hurry!

SERVICE

136

Well I'm...!

Odd! All very odd!...

HIC

HIC

JAMES

A few minutes later...

Suf...Sur...Syb... Ah, here it is! Syldavia: a State in the Balkan Peninsula. In the XIIth century Syldavia was conquered by the Bordurians

RRRRING
RRRRING
RRRRING

Hello?...Yes, it's me...Yes of course it's me...I...Who are you?... What? You'll tell me later?... Can you come and see me? What about?... Oh!... All right, I'll expect you about half past eight... Goodbye...

A man with a foreign accent, with something very important to tell me...?

HIC

In 1275 the people of Syldavia rose against the Bordurians, and in 1277 the revolutionary leader, Baron Almaszout, was proclaimed King. He adopted the title of Ottokar the First, but should not be confused with Premysl Ottakar the First, the duke who became King of Bohemia in the XIIth century

HIC

Twenty past eight. My mysterious foreigner should soon be here.

TINTIN

RRRING

HIC

?

No one there!

Let's look out of the window!...

I say, Tintin, my hiccups have gone!

I really must get this window mended!...

SMASH

No one there, of course!...

I'd better do something about this poor chap.

I must get him on to the sofa.

You know he said his door would always be open to us ...

I'd better shut the door first...

You have a fine way of welcoming people!... Oho! What's all this?

?

Help me to lift him on to the sofa, would you?...

Is he... dead?

But tell us what happened.

No, he's alive; his heart is beating.

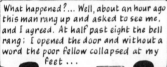

What happened?... Well, about an hour ago this man rang up and asked to see me, and I agreed. At half past eight the bell rang; I opened the door and without a word the poor fellow collapsed at my feet...

Hmm!...

You said, 'without a word'... In that case, how do you know that this was the man who telephoned?...

I don't know, but it seemed likely...

And what about all this evidence of a struggle?

Evidence of a struggle, my foot! The only struggle I had was with the window, which wouldn't open! You aren't trying to say that I knocked this man out?

I didn't say that, but...

Excuse me, gentlemen...

May I ask what I am doing here?...

I rather think I should be asking you that question...

To begin with, can you describe your assailant?

My assailant?... What assailant?

Now don't try any funny business with us, my friend... Come on, what's your name?

I... let's see... It's really very odd, but I... I can't remember!...

139

For the last time, my man, don't try any funny business with us... What's your name?

Out with it!... And get a move on!

What if he's telling the truth and he really is suffering from amnesia?

What has anaemia to do with it?...

Amnesia!... He probably had a violent shock that made him lose his memory! It's always happening. If I were you I'd take him to a hospital and let a doctor have a look at him...

Hmm!...What do you think?...

Hmm!... We could try...

You know, I can't really believe in this magnesia...

It's all very odd... I just can't make head or tail of this business...

Anyway, I'd better get a new window pane put in...

Hello, is that the builder?... Could you replace a pane of glass for me? Yes ...Tintin...You'll come tonight?... Splendid!..

RRRRRING

Oh, it's you! Come in.

Thanks

There...

Goodnight Mr. Tintin. Always glad to help!...

Glad to help!... Not again for a long time, I hope...

!?! ?...! SMASH

Nobody... The street's quite empty..

Ah! There's a note tied to this stone..

For the last time : mind your own business !

'For the last time'... In other words, 'we have already warned you'. But when?... Why, that must have been a warning at the 'Klow'. Of course... they were Syldavians! I've got an idea!... What if I become the professor's secretary and go with him to Syldavia ?...

Next day ...

Bad news !... That Tintin went to see Professor Alembick this morning and agreed to go with him to Syldavia as his secretary!... He's busy getting his passport now. If he goes with the professor our plan is bound to fail !...

You'd better leave this to me; I'll see that Tintin doesn't go!

Some hours later...

Mr. Tintin ?... He's gone out.

What's that, my boy ?

It's a parcel for Mr. Tintin.

Give me that. We'll wait for Tintin up-stairs, and give him this ourselves...

But...

That's enough: we're the police!

Look, there's a letter with the parcel ... Should we open it ?...

'If you want an explanation of yesterday's events, you will find it in this parcel. A Friend.'

Excellent !... What a stroke of luck. Now we shall find something interesting...

There are two men waiting in your room; they told me they were from the police...

Oh?.. Good!

I wonder what they've got to tell me ...

BOOM

!?

141

There it goes!

BOOM

?

What have you done? What's happened?...

Er... there was a parcel for you...

... and a letter... Here: read it... We opened the parcel. We heard a 'fizz' and we just had time to throw it away, or it would have blown up in our faces!

Let's get nearer; we can mix with the crowd...

A bomb!... The cunning scoundrels!...They wanted to kill me!

!?

Quick, downstairs!...The men who did it are out there!...

Hurry! Hurry!

There they are!

It's him!

142

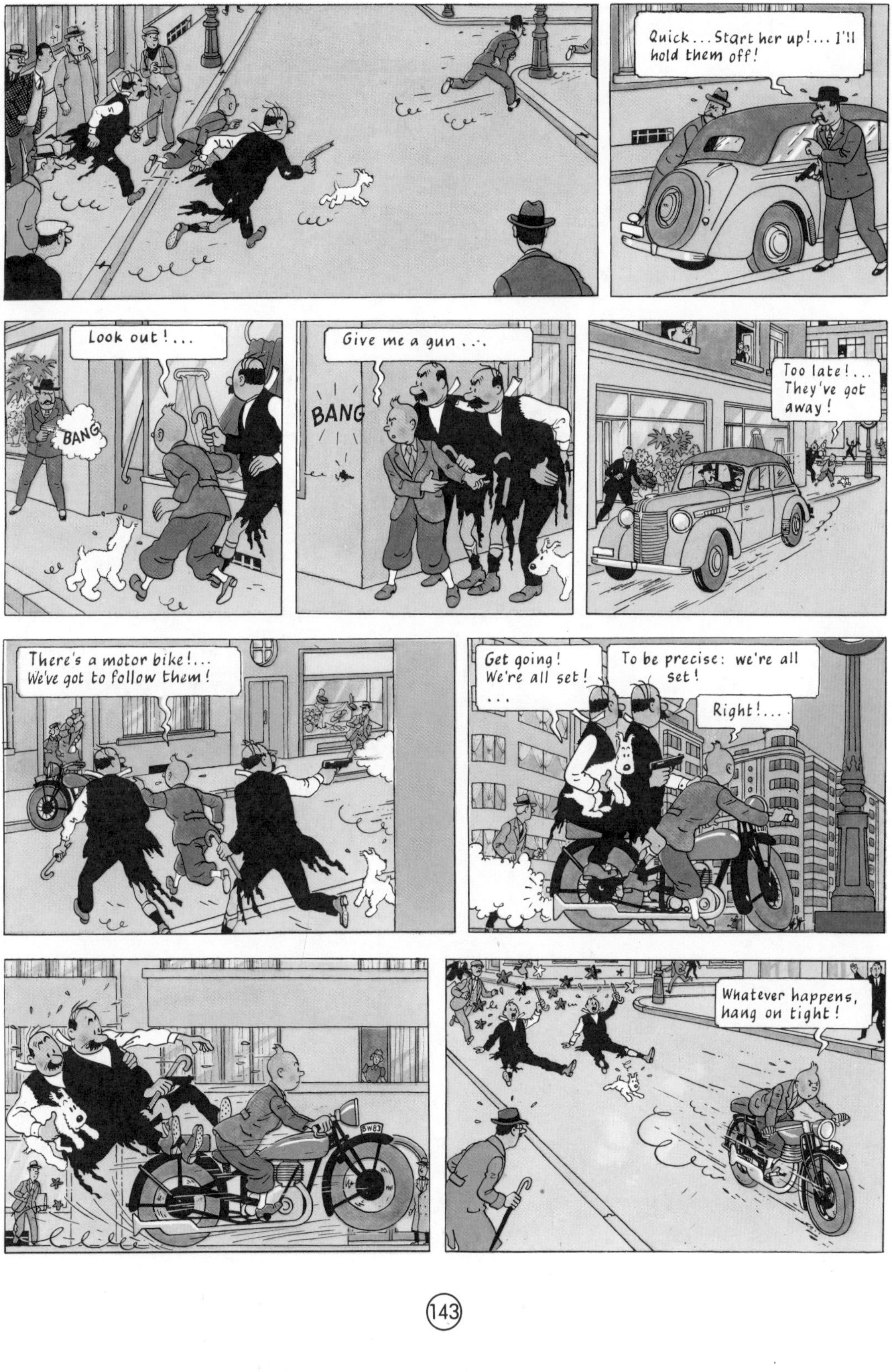

Quick... Start her up!... I'll hold them off!
Look out!...
BANG
Give me a gun...
BANG
Too late!... They've got away!
There's a motor bike!... We've got to follow them!
Get going! We're all set! ...
To be precise: we're all set!
Right!...
BW83
Whatever happens, hang on tight!

He's alone!...We'll fix him!...Let him gradually close up on us...

We're catching up!

Now we've got 'em!...

Now then, jam on the brakes ...Wham!...

!?

This time I think we've really shaken him off for good.

Where's Snowy?...And the others?...What's happened to them?

It can't be true! Surely... yes, it's them! ...Where have they come from?

You started off so suddenly that we... we couldn't keep up with you. So we commandeered this car. Shall we follow them?...

It's no good: they're too far ahead.

I'll leave you here. I must go and pack my things at once. I am going to Syldavia tomorrow.

RRRRING
RRRRING
RRRRING
RRRRING

Hello?...Yes... Ah, good-evening, Professor... Yes, everything is ready for our trip... Yes, I have booked seats on the Klow plane...We'll meet at the airport in the morning, at 11 o'clock...

We go via Prague, yes...Well, goodbye till tomorrow, Professor.. Yes... I... Hello?... Hello?... Hello?...

Ooooh... Help!... Help!... Aaaaaah!...

The professor is in danger! Quick! quick! There's not a moment to lose!...

I only hope I'm not too late!...

?¡※!¿:※∗!

Ah! It's you, Tintin. Come to help me my packing?... Have you finish

I ... I'm sorry, but I don't understand!... I thought I heard you cry out and shout for help...So I rushed straight round...

Me shouting for help?.. I'm afraid I don't know what you're talking about.

But it's extraodinary!... I can't have been dreaming! ..I quite definitely heard shouts for help...

Next morning...

It's very kind of you to come and see me off.

But of course we've come...

To be precise: of course...

Professor, may I introduce Mr. Thomson and Mr. Thompson, of the C.I.D. ... Professor Alembick, sigillographer.

How do you do?

Very well, thank you.

Oh, you've got new hats?

Yes, aren't they smart?... Pure English felt, extra-light: only £3-95. Wonderful bar——gain!

All passengers for Prague, this way please...

Well, goodbye, and bon voyage!...

And good luck in Syldavia!

Thanks.

Compression! Petrol on! Contact!

Come and look what a pretty picture these sheep make... down in that field.

Can you see them, down there?

Yes... How tiny they are: you can hardly see them...

?

How odd...

Are we landing?...

Yes: it's Frankfurt. They touch down for a few minutes.

Mr. Alembick? There's a telegram for you.

Aha!...

Here's some good news... The Syldavian government has put a special aircraft at our disposal. Look...

'Professor Alembick, passenger aboard aircraft No. S73 OO-AGE. Frankfurt Airport. Special plane for Klow will meet you at Prague. Stop. Best wishes.'... It's signed Schzlozitch, Air Minister...

Sweets... Sandwiches... Chocolates... Cigarettes...

I think they're calling us...

?

All passengers for Prague, please take your seats in the aircr aft...

OO-AGE

It's really very odd...

Oh, well, let's forget it and look at this brochure...

COME TO SYLDAVI

SYLDAVIA
KINGDOM OF THE
BLACK PELICAN

SYLDAVIA
THE KINGDOM OF THE BLACK PELICAN

MONG the many enchanting places which deservedly attract foreign visitors with a love for picturesque ceremony and colourful folklore, there is one small country which, although relatively unknown, surpasses many others in interest. Isolated until modern times because of its inaccessible position, this country is now served by a regular air-line network, which brings it within the reach of all who love unspoiled beauty, the proverbial hospitality of a peasant people, and the charm of medieval customs which still survive despite the march of progress.

This is Syldavia.

Syldavia is a small country in Eastern Europe, comprising two great valleys: those of the river Vladir, and its tributary, the Moltus. The rivers meet at Klow, the capital (122,000 inhabitants). These valleys are flanked by wide plateaux covered with forests, and are surrounded by high, snow-capped mountains. In the fertile Syldavian plains are corn-lands and cattle pastures. The subsoil is rich in minerals of all kinds.

Numerous thermal and sulphur springs gush from the earth, the chief centres being at Klow (cardiac diseases) and Kragoniedin (rheumatic complaints).

The total population is estimated to be 642,000 inhabitants.

Syldavia exports wheat, mineral-water from Klow, firewood, horses and violinists.

HISTORY OF SYLDAVIA

Until the VIth century, Syldavia was inhabited by nomadic tribes of unknown origin.

Overrun by the Slavs in the VIth century, the country was conquered in the Xth century by the Turks, who drove the Slavs into the mountains and occupied the plains.

In 1127, Hveghi, leader of a Slav tribe, swooped down from the mountains at the head of a band of partisans and fell upon isolated Turkish villages, putting all who resisted him to the sword. Thus he rapidly became master of a large part of Syldavian territory.

A great battle took place in the valley of the Moltus near Zileheroum, the Turkish capital of Syldavia, between the Turkish army and Hveghi's irregulars.

Enfeebled by long inactivity and badly led by incompetent officers, the Turkish army put up little resistance and fled in disorder.

Having vanquished the Turks, Hveghi was elected king, and given the name Muskar, that is, The Brave (Muskh: 'brave' and Kar: 'king').

The capital, Zileheroum, was renamed Klow, that is, Freetown, (Kloho: 'to free', and Ow: 'town').

A typical fisherman from Dbrnouk (south coast of Syldavia)

Guard at the Royal Treasure House, Klow

◀ *Syldavian peasant on her way to market*

A view of Niedzdrow, in the Vladir valley ▶

THE BATTLE OF ZILEHEROUM

After a XVth century miniature

H.M. King Muskar XII, the present ruler of Syldavia in the uniform of Colonel of the Guards

struck him a blow on the head with the sceptre, laying him low and at the same time crying in Syldavian: '*Eih bennek, eih blavek!*', which can be said to mean: 'If you gather thistles, expect prickles'. And turning to his astonished court he said: '*Honi soit qui mal y pense!*'

Then, gazing intently at his sceptre, he addressed it in the following words: 'O Sceptre, thou hast saved my life. Be henceforward the true symbol of Syldavian Kingship. Woe to the king who loses thee, for I declare that such a man shall be unworthy to rule thereafter.'

And from that time, every year on St. Vladimir's Day each successor of Ottokar IV has made a great ceremonial tour of his capital.

He bears in his hand the historic sceptre, without which he would lose the right to rule; as he passes, the people sing the famous anthem:

Syldavians unite!
Praise our King's might:
The Sceptre his right!

Right: The sceptre of Ottokar IV

Below: An illuminated page from 'The Memorable Deeds of Ottokar IV', a XIVth century manuscript

Muskar was a wise king who lived at peace with his neighbours, and the country prospered. He died in 1168, mourned by all his subjects.

His eldest son succeeded to the throne with the title of Muskar II.

Unlike his father, Muskar II lacked authority and was unable to keep order in his kingdom. A period of anarchy replaced one of peaceful prosperity.

In the neighbouring state of Borduria the people observed Syldavia's decline, and their king profited by this opportunity to invade the country. Borduria annexed Syldavia in 1195.

For almost a century Syldavia groaned under the foreign yoke.

In 1275 Baron Almaszout repeated the exploits of Hveghi by coming down from the hills and routing the Bordurians in less than six months.

He was proclaimed King in 1277, taking the name of Ottokar. He was, however, much less powerful than Muskar.

The barons who had helped him in the campaign against the Bordurians forced him to grant them a charter, based on the English Magna Carta signed by King John (Lackland). This marked the beginning of the feudal system in Syldavia.

Ottokar I of Syldavia should not be confused with the Ottokars (Premysls) who were Dukes, and later Kings, of Bohemia.

This period was noteworthy for the rise in power of the nobles, who fortified their castles and maintained bands of armed mercenaries, strong enough to oppose the King's forces.

But the true founder of the kingdom of Syldavia was Ottokar IV, who ascended the throne in 1370.

From the time of his accession he initiated widespread reforms. He raised a powerful army and subdued the arrogant nobles, confiscating their wealth.

He fostered the advancement of the arts, of letters, commerce and agriculture.

He united the whole nation and gave it that security, both at home and abroad, so necessary for the renewal of prosperity.

It was he who pronounced those famous words: '*Eih bennek, eih blavek*', which have become the motto of Syldavia.

The origin of this saying is as follows:

One day Baron Staszrvich, son of one of the dispossessed nobles whose lands had been forfeited to the crown, came before the sovereign and recklessly claimed the throne of Syldavia.

The King listened in silence, but when the presumptuous baron's speech ended with a demand that he deliver up his sceptre, the King rose and cried fiercely: 'Come and get it!'

Mad with rage, the young baron drew his sword, and before the retainers could intervene, fell upon the King.

The King stepped swiftly aside, and as his adversary passed him, carried forward by the impetus of his charge, Ottokar

Well, that's all very interesting, but ...

...I must be on my guard. Without his glasses this man can pick out a flock of sheep from as high up as this. He has good eyes for a short-sighted person!... And another strange thing ever since I found him packing his bags I haven't seen him smoke a single cigarette

...Unless I'm very much mistaken, I'm travelling with an impostor!... If that's so, then everything fits in... The shouts I heard on the telephone were from the real Professor Alembick. He has been kidnapped and this man has taken his place

He must be exposed! At Prague I'll pull off that false beard, and have him arrested!

Prague?... Already?

Yes, we are landing...

Now's my chance!

OH!

OUCH!

?

I...I'm sorry...I ...I missed a step ...I beg your pardon ...

D-don't mention it!.

Professor Alembick?... Your special plane is wait-...ing.

It's a real beard !

But what about his glasses? ...Not that that proves anything. Plenty of people can see better at a distance than near to... As for the cigarettes, perhaps he has simply given up smoking ...

You see, Snowy, in rough weather when the plane bumps about you fasten yourself into the seat like this...

There is the frontier... We are now over Syldavia...

What lovely country..

Very pretty, isn't it? I'll let you admire it a bit more closely...

There!... Happy landings!...

TINTIN?!

Quick, the parachute!...

No time to buckle it on!...

Mind the jerk when it opens!...

Zrälükz!...

Wooah!

Czesztot on klebcz !

? ?

?

Splendid !...
Snowy fell into
the parachute.
.. He's safe !

My aeroplane... BRRRR... I fell... Crash!... Into the straw...

Czestot wzryzkar nietz on vaghabontz! ...Czestot bätczer yhzer kzömmetz noh dascz politzski?...

Snowy! Snowy!

Wooah! Wooah!

Kzommet micz omhz, noh dascz politzski!

Come with you to the police?... With pleasurski! ...I've got a complaint to make!

ГЕПОЛИЦКИ

Captain, what I have to say is of the utmost importance... May I speak to you in private?...

Er... Yes... Leave us alone...

First, may I ask you a question?... I read in a brochure about Syldavia that if your King loses his sceptre he will be forced to abdicate. Is that true?...

As a matter of fact it is... But how does this concern you?

I'll tell you. I am certain there's a conspiracy against King Muskar XII, and that certain people will try to steal the sceptre from him!

What's that you say?... What makes you imagine such a thing?

I'll explain... But first, are you sure we are not overheard?

Definitely not. Go on...

This must be serious. They've been in there nearly an hour...

АДВИЧА

You have just rendered a great service to my country: I thank you. I will telegraph at once to Klow and have Professor Alembick arrested. I'm sure I can rely on you for absolute secrecy..

Of course... But I must be on my way ... Can I hire a car?

There isn't a single car in the village. But tomorrow is market-day in Klow. You can go with a peasant who is leaving here today. But you won't arrive there until morning...

Too bad, but I have no choice. I'll go with the peasant

Hello?... Yes, this is Klow 3324... Yes, Central Committee... Trovik speaking...Oh it's you Wizskitotz... What?... Tintin?...But that's impossible: the pilot has just told me... What?...Into some straw!...Szplug! He must be prevented from reaching Klow at all costs!... Do it how you like... Yes, ring up Sirov...

Hello?...Yes, this is Sirov... Hello Wizskitotz...Yes...A young boy, on the road to Klow... In a peasant's cart... Good, we'll be waiting in the forest...Yes, we'll leave at once... Goodbye!...

Look out!... Here they come!...

Hands up!...

?

Where's the young foreigner you are taking to Klow?...

Th–th– the young f-f-f-foreign...-er...

That's enough!... We know he's with you!... Search the cart, Zlop!

Th-th-the f-f-foreign...er who..who w-w-w

Was w-w-w-with m-m-me?...

What makes you stutter like that?... Fear?...

N-n-no! ...It...it...it... it's b-b-be-because...I...I... I t-t-talk...talk...talk...

Sirov! There's no one there!

!

Szplug! Where can he be?... Come on, are you going to talk?...

I...I...w-was g-g-going t-t-to t-tell y-y-you, b-b-bbut y-yyou in-in-inter-inter-interrupted m-m-me!.. He st-st-stopped at... at...at... th-th-the Co-co-co–

Cocoa!...Cocoa!...What cocoa?.. Have you been drinking?...

The Co-co-coach-Coachman's Rest, an-an-and ...

Why didn't you say so sooner? ...

Quiet!...I can hear a car!

An-an-and he... he...he... g-g-g-

If you say one word, or make one move...just remember our rifles are trained on you!...

L-l-l-listen ...l...l...I'm I'm...

It's gone... We can go back...

I...I'm t-t-try-trying to t-t-tell...yy-yy-yyou...th-th-the y-y-young f-f-for-foreigner w-w-

Szplitz on Szplug! Where is he?...

W-w-was in...in...in th-th-that c-c-car w-w-w-which j-j-just papa-papa-passed!...

! ! !

Yes, I am singing tonight at the Winter Garden in Klow... Would you like to hear me now?...

I'd love to.

Ah, ♫ my beauty ♪ past compare: these jewels ♫ bright I wear!...

Was I ever Margar-i-i-ta? ♫

It's lucky the windows are strong!

Hello?...Yes, this is Wizskitotz...Ah, it's you Sirov...Well?...What?...Szplug! ...So it's not your fault?...Perhaps you think it's mine, eh?...What?...If he hadn't stuttered so?...If!...If!...You can get round anything with 'if'...I'll telephone to the Chief of Police at Zlip...Yes, he's one of us...He'll stop him on the road.

Well, how did you like that?...

V-very much indeed!...

In that case, just to please you I'll sing something else!

Where is the boy who is travelling with you?...

He got out earlier on. He'd forgotten something at the Coachman's Rest, so he went back...

I would have given any excuse to escape!

Meanwhile, in Klow...
So, you wish to have access to the Treasure House to examine the national archives?...I won't conceal from you that this is a privilege rarely accorded to a foreigner, but since our ambassador has vouched for you, I think His Majesty will look favourably upon your request

That's him... We'll ask for his papers...

Your papers are not in order! ... Come with us to the police station!

Quite correct: your papers are not in order!... I shall have to keep you here until I receive instructions

But Captain, there must be some mistake!... My passport was stamped before I left and...

I am sorry, but I cannot allow you to proceed. Take him away!

Captain!... You must listen!... I have something important to tell you!... I...

Hello?... Wizskitotz?... This is Szplodj... I've got our fine bird!...Yes, we simply picked him up... Now what do you want us to do with him?... Yes...Yes... He obviously mustn't get to Klow... I'll think it over...That's it, ring up in the morning...Goodbye...

While I cool my heels here, goodness knows what's going on in Klow...

Aaaouaaah!...It's getting dark... I'd better try and get some sleep, as there's nothing else to do...

This is Radio Klow... We are now broadcasting a concert from the Winter Garden at Klow. The soloist is Signora Bianca Castafiore of La Scala, Milan.

♪ ♫ ❋ ＊ ♪ ♯ ❋ ♫ ♪

Ah, my beauty ♪ past compare; these jewels bright I wear! ♪ ♪ Was I ever Margarita?

Is it I? ♪ Come reply! ♪ Mirror, mirror tell me truly! ♫♫ ♩

Next day...

This document bearing the royal signature will admit you to the Treasure Chamber. Lieutenant Kromir will escort you there...

The regalia is housed in the keep of Kropow Castle. A special guard is mounted over it.

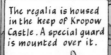

In the name of the King! Professor, please come with me.

The regalia seems well guarded!

It is! The man who is clever enough to steal it hasn't been born!

There is His Majesty's regalia, Professor!...

160

And this is the Muniments Room, which adjoins the Treasure Chamber. You must forgive me, but two guards will remain with you for as long as you are here. The doors will also be locked from the outside. Those are the orders. I hope you will not be offended.

Not in the least...

Meanwhile...

You are to take this young man to Klow. But be careful!... He is a dangerous ruffian who has been meddling in State secrets... In fact, I've been given to understand, on high authority, that it'd be a good thing if he never arrived in Klow

These are your orders... You, as the driver, will stage a breakdown. You will get out to look at the engine, and the others will follow... The prisoner will then try to escape and ... You understand me?

Yes, sir!... But what if he doesn't try to get away?

Don't worry!... He will!...

I wonder who can have sent me this?... A friend? ... What friend?...

BEWARE!
YOU ARE GOING TO BE TAKEN TO KLOW TO BE SHOT! YOU MUST TRY TO ESCAPE. ON THE JOURNEY, PRETEND TO BE ASLEEP. THE DRIVER, WHO IS A FRIEND, WILL STAGE A BREAKDOWN AND CALL THE OTHER GUARDS AWAY. THAT WILL BE THE MOMENT FOR YOU TO MAKE YOUR ESCAPE.

A FRIEND

We'd better get rid of this, in case I'm searched.

Here, Snowy, swallow this paper pellet for me...

Hurry up now, Snowy, I think someone is coming for us...

I suppose you think it's easy?

Why have you stopped?...

It's the engine...

Let's have a look... Oh, it's all right: he's asleep...

Look out, he's moving! ...He's getting out... Get ready...

A trap!... I'm done for!

There he goes!... Don't miss!...

There's only one way: a nose-dive!...Whoops!

BANG BANG BANG

WHIZZ

BANG

WHIZZ

CRACK

It's no good, hold your fire!...He's disappeared behind the boulders! ...He must have broken his neck... but we'd better look for him...

He fell down there ...somewhere behind those rocks...

They're coming!...

Careful! About here...

Szplug! Where is he? We've simply got to find him...The captain will never forgive us if we let him get away, after he'd planned that trap...

Come on, let's have another look. He can't be far away...

Whew!... They've passed us...

Now, off we go to Klow!...

I must watch my step!...I see that no one can be trusted!...I must warn the King himself.

Meanwhile in Klow...

I wonder if I might be permitted to photograph some of the documents?

As a rule that is not allowed, but His Majesty might consent...

Ah! Here's the main road again.

Golly, I'm hungry...

You have His Majesty's permission to photograph the documents. But the pictures may only be taken by the official Court Photographer, Herr Czarlitz. Here is the order which authorises him to go with you into the castle...

Klow at last!...

When are we going to eat?

Which way to the palace, please?

Follow this street to Ottokar Square, then turn left...

DANGER HIGH VOLTAGE

What a downpour! We'll shelter until this is over...

Is this a restaurant?

It's stopping now...

Come on Snowy!...We must hurry to warn the King of the danger he's in...

Hurry up, Snowy! Hey, where is Snowy?

Snowy!... Snowy!... Snowy! ..

They have wonderful bones in this country, Tintin!...

?

?

DIPLODOCUS GIGANTICUS

You take that bone back where you found it, at once! You understand...And be quick!...

Ah! There's the palace!

Could His Majesty grant me an audience?...I have most important and urgent business...

Please wait here: I will see if His Majesty's aide-de-camp will see you. Whom shall I announce?...

Tintin.

Mr. Tintin?...On important business?...All right, show him in.

Certainly, Signora...Yes...yes...tonight, at half-past eight...His Majesty will be delighted...Your servant, Signora...

Meanwhile...

So that's all arranged, Herr Czarlitz...I will come and fetch you in the morning at about nine, and we will go to Kropow Castle together...

Very good, Professor.

So you want an audience with His Majesty?... May I ask why?...

Er... I... you must excuse me, but... it is highly confidential....

Sir, I am His Majesty's aide-de-camp!... I venture to say that my sovereign places complete trust in me!

I do not doubt it, Colonel!... But the news I have to communicate to the King is so serious that it is for his ears alone.

Very well, I will not insist... Will you come back tonight, at about half past eight? I will try and arrange for His Majesty to allow you a few minutes, before his reception at the palace...

Thank you very much.

Now for a meal, Snowy!

Hello?... Yes, this is the Central Committee. Ah, it's you, Boris. What's the latest news? ...Yes...What?...Tintin?... Are you sure? But the Chief of Police at Zlip has just sworn that... Yes...Terribly important information

But he didn't say what it was?.. Good!...Aha!...He'll be back tonight at eight-thirty?...That's fine, it gives us time...Listen, he must not speak to the King.. .. Definitely not!... This is what we'll do: listen...

That evening...

The King is willing to grant you a short interview. Please go with the Captain of the Guard and he will take you to the Audience Chamber. His Majesty will see you there.

Thank you.

Ssh!... Here they come...

Wooah! Wooah!

?

That mongrel has given us away!...Come on!..

An ambush!...

Got you, my friend. Don't try to resist!...

!

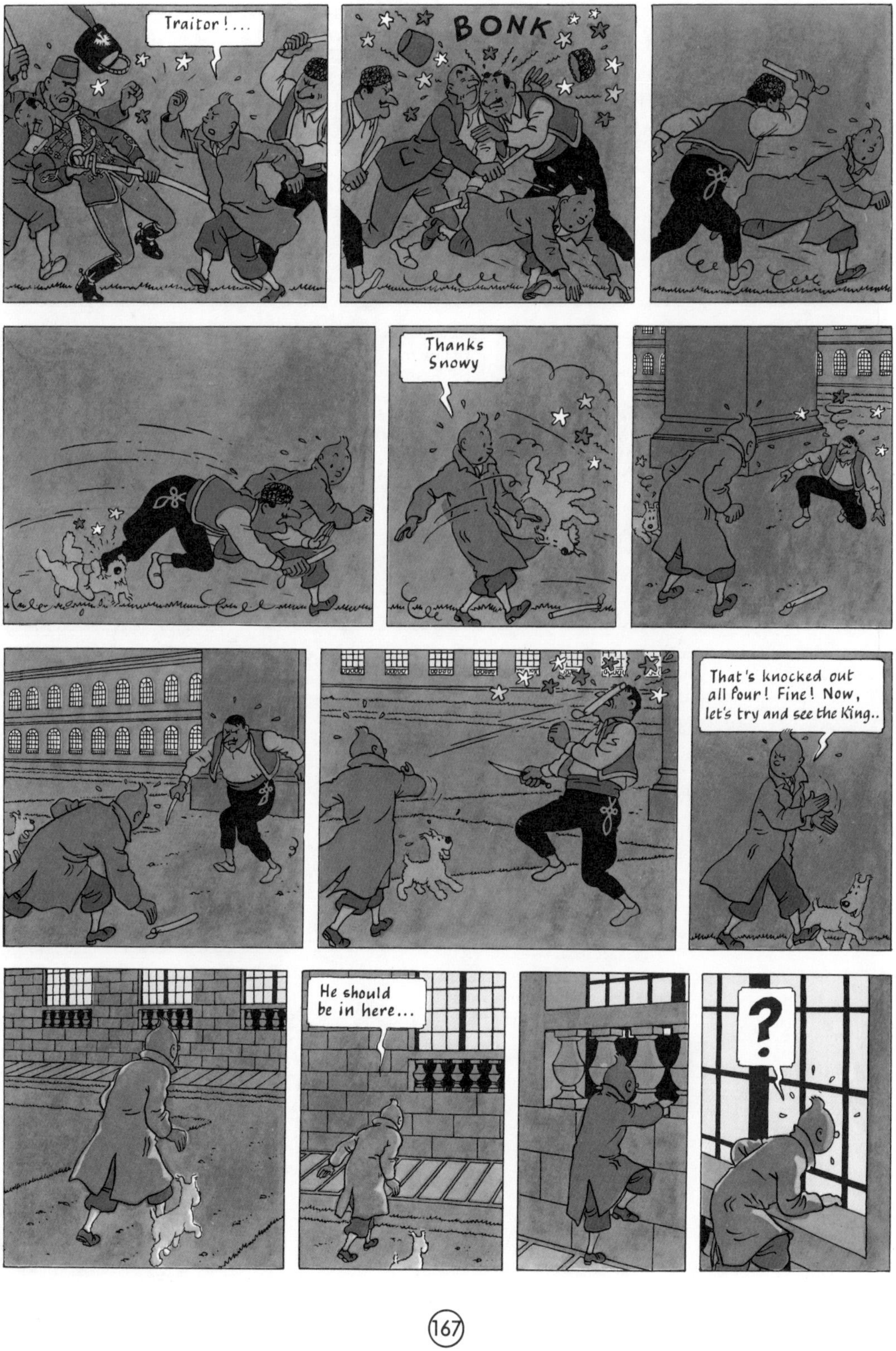
Traitor!...
BONK
Thanks Snowy
That's knocked out all four! Fine! Now, let's try and see the King..
He should be in here...
?

Ah, my beauty past ♫ compare; ♪ these jewels bright I wear ♫♪

CRASH

Quick, it came from the conservatory, outside the Audience Chamber.

The Guard!...There isn't a minute to lose!...

Let me go!... Let me go!... I must speak to the King!..

Your Majesty! Take care! ... Don't trust the prof...

The Guard!... Call the Guard! ... Hurry!

...It was only a young anarchist who managed to get into the palace, Sire...

Next morning..

More time wasted!... And I'm sure the conspirators won't be wasting theirs! ...

CLINK CLINK CLINK

You are being transferred to the State Prison to await trial. Come with us. The police van is outside...

Hello, this is St. Vladimir's Hospital... An accident?... ....Casualties? In Moltus Street? ...All right, I'll send an ambulance

This one still hasn't come round...

Yes, definitely suffering from concussion...

We'd better go back for the others...

A very useful thing, concussion ... Come on, Snowy! Now or never ...

Aha! That's done the trick!... Now back to the palace!

I must see the King at all costs.

This time nothing is going to stop me speaking to him!...

A-11

169

You aren't hurt, I hope?

No, thank you. I'm all right... Great snakes!.. The King!

Take care, Sire!... This is the young anarchist who tri—ed...

?

Don't shoot, Sir!... Please listen!... I am not an anarchist. I wanted to warn you... Even at this moment those scoundrels may be trying to steal your sceptre!

What do you mean?

It's the truth, Sir. I am certain that Professor Alembick is an impostor. Coming to Syldavia to study the archives was only a blind. He and his accomplices plan to steal King Ottokar's sceptre, and so force you to give up your throne!

By Vladimir! Can it be?

Meanwhile...

And this man is in with them, Sir... That is why he tried to stop me speaking to you!...

He's in the plot too?

It's a lie, Sire!

He is lying, Sire, and I will...

You will return to the palace at once and await my orders! ... I myself will go to Kropow Castle with this young man and prove for myself the truth of his allegations!...

We must hurry, Sir... I'm sure there's not a moment to lose...

That's that... May we now go into the Treasure Chamber, and photograph the crown and sceptre?...

Certainly.

The light is not very good. We'll have to use a flash-bulb...

We're nearly there... Those are the towers of Kropow Castle... the sceptre is in the keep, that square tower in the centre... I only hope we're not too late!...

The King!...

Everything seems quite normal... We are in time!

I hope so, Sir...

Where is Professor Alembick?

In the Treasure Chamber, Sire, with the Governor of the Castle and Herr Czarlitz...

Open up! In the name of the King!

No answer! Quick, bring me the other keys!

Could it really be possible?

Let us hope not, Sir... Ah! Here is the guard with the keys.

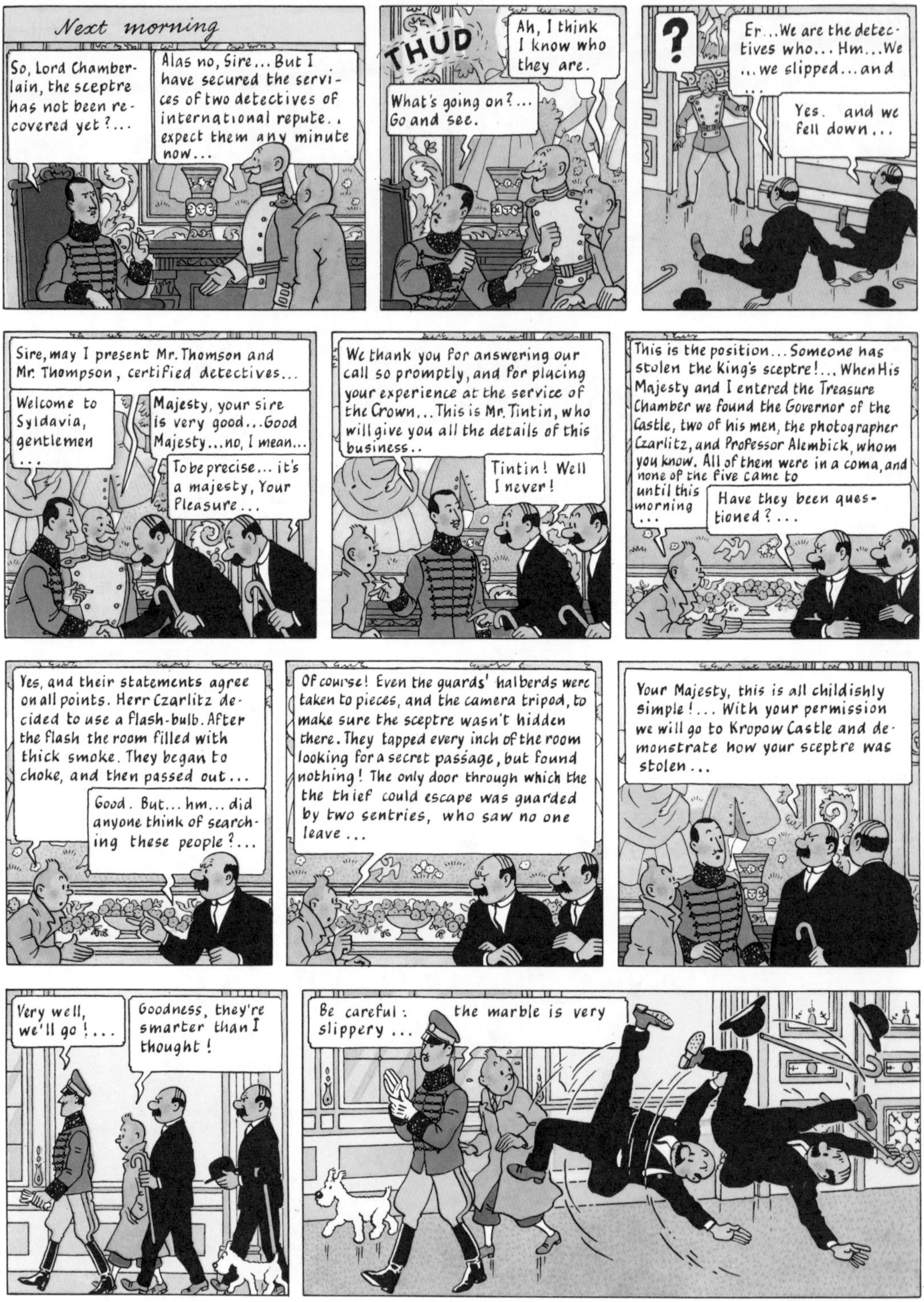
Next morning
So, Lord Chamberlain, the sceptre has not been recovered yet?...
Alas no, Sire... But I have secured the services of two detectives of international repute.. expect them any minute now...
THUD
Ah, I think I know who they are.
What's going on?... Go and see.
?
Er...We are the detectives who... Hm...We ...we slipped...and ...
Yes. and we fell down...
Sire, may I present Mr. Thomson and Mr. Thompson, certified detectives...
Welcome to Syldavia, gentlemen ...
Majesty, your sire is very good...Good Majesty...no, I mean...
To be precise... it's a majesty, Your Pleasure...
We thank you for answering our call so promptly, and for placing your experience at the service of the Crown... This is Mr. Tintin, who will give you all the details of this business..
Tintin! Well I never!
This is the position... Someone has stolen the King's sceptre!... When His Majesty and I entered the Treasure Chamber we found the Governor of the Castle, two of his men, the photographer Czarlitz, and Professor Alembick, whom you know. All of them were in a coma, and none of the five came to until this morning ...
Have they been questioned?...
Yes, and their statements agree on all points. Herr Czarlitz decided to use a flash-bulb. After the flash the room filled with thick smoke. They began to choke, and then passed out...
Good. But... hm... did anyone think of searching these people?...
Of course! Even the guards' halberds were taken to pieces, and the camera tripod, to make sure the sceptre wasn't hidden there. They tapped every inch of the room looking for a secret passage, but found nothing! The only door through which the the thief could escape was guarded by two sentries, who saw no one leave...
Your Majesty, this is all childishly simple!... With your permission we will go to Kropow Castle and demonstrate how your sceptre was stolen...
Very well, we'll go!...
Goodness, they're smarter than I thought!
Be careful: the marble is very slippery...

This is the Treasure Chamber. The sceptre was here...

As we said, Your Majesty: the whole thing is childishly simple!

This is what happened. One of the five people present was in the plot. He collapsed when the smoke was released, but took care to hold a handkerchief to his nose. When he was sure the others had been put to sleep he got up, opened the glass case, seized the sceptre, opened the window and dropped the sceptre into the courtyard. There an accomplice collected it, took it away, and that was that!

Impossible, gentlemen! The courtyard is guarded. No one goes there but the sentries; and the sentries are above suspicion... They are men of absolute trust who would die rather than betray their King!

As a matter of fact the guard patrolling this side of the tower did hear a window open and shut. But he did not notice anything unusual ...

Exactly!... Because the thief must have thrown the sceptre over the ramparts surrounding the castle!... An accomplice waited there, picked it up, and made off.

However, you shall see... Could you get me something the same size as the sceptre?...

Certainly...

But look! It is at least a hundred yards from this window to the ramparts! ...And there are bars...

What do they matter?... It just needs a good aim...

There... Will this do?...

Perfectly

Now I'll show you ...

? BONG

Clumsy oaf!... Let me show you the right way to do it!...

Watch carefully!...

BONG ?

You can see for yourselves that the sceptre didn't leave this room like that!...

Yes...Yes...maybe. Anyway, we'd like to question Alembick and Czarlitz...

Sire!... Sire!... Ah, at last I've found you...

?

Sire!... It's unbelievable!... Professor Alembick and Herr Czarlitz...

...have escaped from the State Prison, Sire... They had accomplices among the warders!... Four of them have disappeared with the fugitives!

By the Sceptre of Ottokar!

Accomplices!... Accomplices!... They are everywhere!... Oh, the plot was well laid: all is lost!

Leave it to us, Your Majesty... It may take a week, a month, even a year, but we will recover your sceptre!...

Alas, gentlemen, there are only three days!... If I am without my sceptre on St. Vladimir's Day, I have no choice but to abdicate!

'Only three days', said Columbus, 'and I will give you a new world!' Only three days, Majesty, and we swear to bring your sceptre, bound hand and foot..

Thank you, gentlemen! May you succeed.

This time our honour is at stake! We have sworn to find the sceptre; we must keep our word!

To be precise: we must keep our word!

St. Vladimir protect them! ... They will succeed, won't they?...

I hope so, Sir, with all my heart!

In any case, I'd like your permission to try to solve this mystery myself.

Thank you, my friend. Whatever happens, I shall never forget what you have done for me!

The vital thing is to find out HOW the sceptre was stolen...

TO

YS

⁉ ⚡!

Eureka!... Eureka!... I've got it!

YS

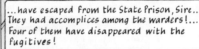

Quick, back to the castle!

I've got it!... Come with me to the Treasure Chamber!... I'll show you!...

Show me what?

How the sceptre was stolen!... Quick! Follow me!

Don't go so fast!... Wait for me!...

Has he gone in?..

Yes, sir...

? OW!

?! !?

?

What happened?... Quick, tell us!...

The camera!... Look at the camera!...

A spring?...

Yes, this spring came out. It hit me in the face and knocked me out!...

It's amazing!... How did you discover that?

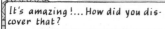

By walking past a toy-shop! ...I saw a little spring gun; it gave me the idea that perhaps the camera was faked up to hide a spring capable of throwing the sceptre beyond the castle ramparts! And my guess was right!...

Watch!... There's the spring back in place... I insert into the tube this stick used by the two detectives...

I place the camera by the window, the forked end of our makeshift sceptre through the bars...

I click the shutter, and ... Whoops!

It's fallen in the wood, beyond the river!... I'm going to have a look round over there.

You will find a boat down by the bank...

176

If that fool Czarlitz had aimed at the clump of birch trees by the river bank as we agreed, we'd have found the sceptre long ago...

!

So they haven't found it yet! ...There's not a moment to lose!...I must get back, and have this wood surrounded.

?

HOORAY!...

Hooray! I've found it!

!

Now, I must give the others the slip...

Crumbs! They've got me!

Yes, got you all right!

The sceptre, Snowy!...Save the sceptre!...

Come here, you mangy cur!... Come here!

Here's the river!... In we go!... Just let them try and catch me!

?

!

BANG BANG

Every man for himself, boys!... The police!...

Poor old Tintin!

Where's the sceptre?

They've got it again!... Snowy dropped it!

Too late!

How did you know I was here?

When we went back to the castle they told us you had crossed the river...

There's the King... They told him, too. He went round by the bridge while we crossed in a boat...

Well, what has happened?...

Those gangsters have got away in a car, with the sceptre! ... If you will lend us your car, Sir, we three will try and catch them...

They haven't got much of a start on us... We'll soon catch them up.

We're almost out of petrol... We'll have to stop at the first pump we come to...

Ah! There's one...

Five gallons!... And make it snappy!...

Another twenty miles to the frontier... Good!...In half an hour we shall be clear of Syldavia, and the sceptre will be safe!

The King's car!... They're after us!

We certainly caught them on the hop!... They've taken to the mountains!

They hadn't even time to get back into their car...

We must hurry!... They musn't get away!

They're still following us...

We must stop this! ... We'll fool them! ...

Come on!... We'll get them!...

BANG

Take cover everybody... They are shooting at us!

BANG

Where have Thomson and Thompson got to?... I can't see them anywhere.

BANG

CRACK

There must be some way of catching them...

Follow me, Snowy, and don't show yourself!... We'll sneak round behind them.

180

Hello, where's the third one?...

Not a sign of life...

Perhaps we hit him!... Look! There are the other two...

Hands up!

Now, I see!... You blocked our way while your pal got away with the sceptre!...

Quick! You look after these thugs!... I'm going on...

Szplug! I can't understand it. ...He's still on my tail!...

It's getting dark... We can't keep this up much longer.

We can't go on now... We'll have to spend the night here!...

We can only wait until it's light...

Next day, at dawn...

Off we go Snowy!... We simply must re-cover the sceptre!

We'll walk fast: That will warm us up...

SYLDAVIA BORDURIA

The frontier at last!...
I'm safe!...

SYLDAVIA BOR

SYLDAVIA

Another yard and
he'd have been over...!

One day you'll break your neck with all those acrobatics!...

Let's search him... Ah! Here's his wallet...

?

Z.Z.R.K. 1239

SECRET To Section Commanders, Shock Troops

SUBJECT: Seizure of Power

I wish to draw your attention to the order in which the operations for seizure of power in Syldavia will take place.

On the eve of St. Vladimir's Day, agents in our propaganda units will foment incidents, and arrange for Bordurian nationals to be beaten up.

On St. Vladimir's Day, at 12 o'clock (H-hour), shock troops will seize Radio Klow, the airfield, the gas works and power station, the banks, the general post office, the Royal Palace, 'kropow Castle, etc...

In due course each section commander will receive precise orders concerning his particular mission.

I salute you!
(signed)
Müsstler.

Z.Z.R.K. 1240

SECRET To Section Commanders, Shock Troops

SUBJECT: Seizure of Power

I wish to remind you that I shall broadcast a call to arms when Radio Klow is in our hands.

Motorized Bordurian troops will then cross into Syldavian territory, to free our native land from the tyranny of King Muskar XII.

Allowing for the feeble resistance they may meet with from a few fanatical royalist partisans and certain subversive sections of the populace, the Bordurian troops will arrive in Klow at about 5.0 p.m.

I call upon all members of Z.Z.R.K. to defend until then, with the last drop of their blood, the positions they will have occupied at midday.

I salute you!
(signed)
Müsstler.

There's no time to lose! We must get back to Klow as fast as we can...

Not on foot I hope?

What's the matter with me?

Oh, I know... I haven't eaten anything since yesterday! If only I had some food!

There's a house over there... But it's across the frontier. Can't be helped... I'm too hungry!

A Bordurian frontier post!...

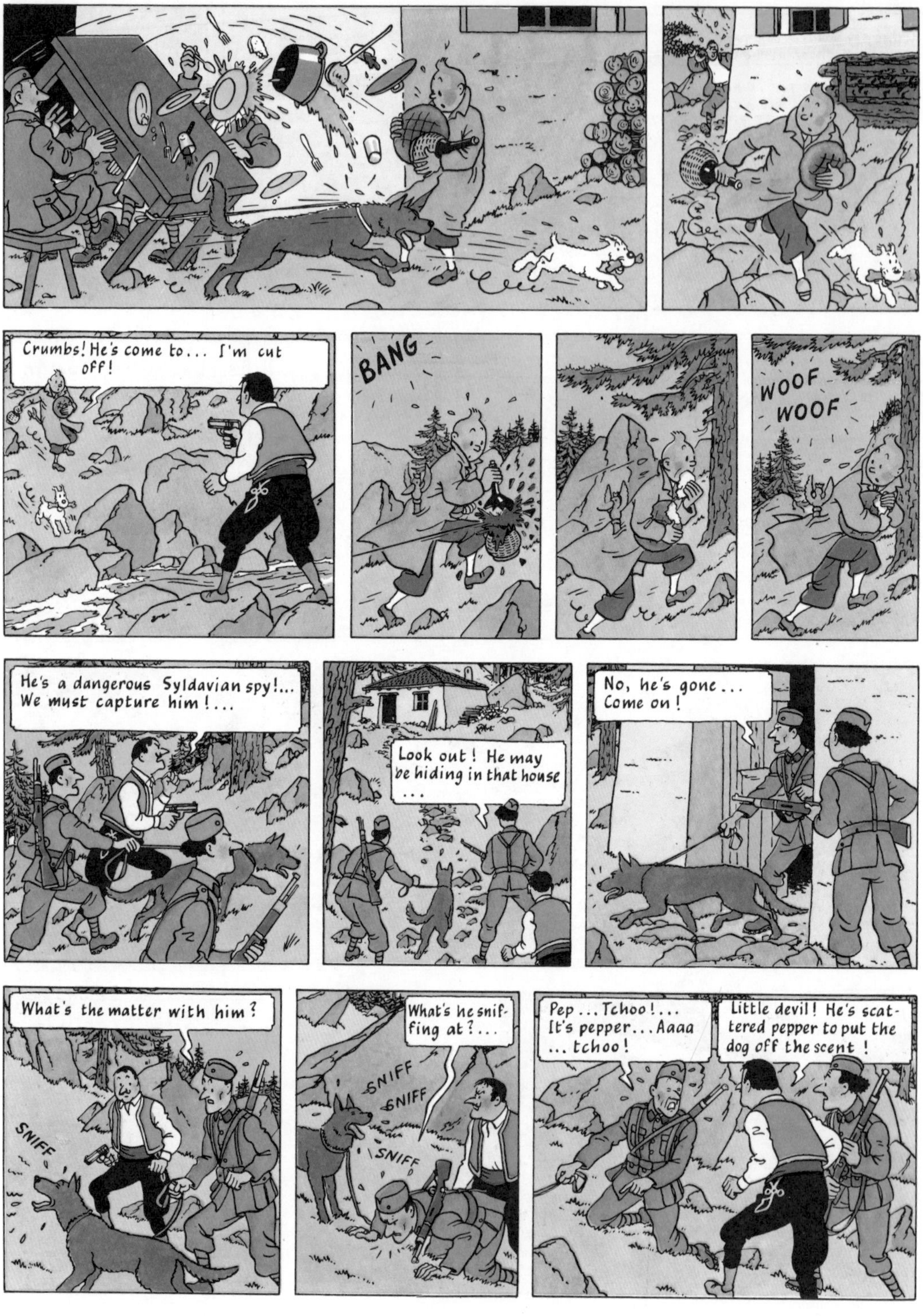

Crumbs! He's come to... I'm cut off!
BANG
WOOF WOOF
He's a dangerous Syldavian spy!... We must capture him!...
Look out! He may be hiding in that house...
No, he's gone... Come on!
What's the matter with him?
SNIFF
What's he sniffing at?...
SNIFF
SNIFF
SNIFF
Pep... Tchoo!... It's pepper... Aaaa... tchoo!
Little devil! He's scattered pepper to put the dog off the scent!

Next day...

That's two nights in the open... I'm tired out!... If I don't find the way soon I'll never get back in time!

A Bordurian fighter!

He's lowered his undercarriage...Where's he landing?

?

If I could grab one of those planes I'd be in Klow in less than an hour...

Everything O.K.?

Yes, nothing unusual ..just reconnaissance along the frontier..

You know, I've been tipped off that Müstler will give his broadcast at midday tomorrow...And an hour later our squadron will land at Klow.

?!*
*!●!

Flat out for Klow!...

It's getting dark...That's annoying. I shan't be there before nightfall...

Hello? Ack-Ack H.Q.?...This is Listening post 34... A Bordurian aircraft has crossed the frontier, heading for Klow ...What shall we do?

You have your orders, Lieutenant. Shoot it down!...

Hello!... Searchlights!

They've picked us up!... I hope they...

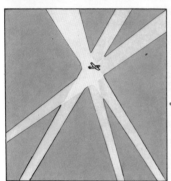

Crumbs!...They're firing...at me!

Got him!... Look, he's on fire...

Ah, a signpost!... That's a stroke of luck!

ISTOW 19½ miles
KLOW 15 ¾ miles

Sixteen miles: that's five hours' walk!...

A mere trifle!

A farm!...Stables!... If only I could borrow a horse...

That's a splendid idea!

Aha, here's a horse!... Whoa there!... Good, here's a saddle too... Whoa now! Gently does it...

On the whole I think we'd better go on foot.

Why not?... A little walk will do us good.

That night...

Things are grave, Sire!... the people are suspicious: there are rumours that the sceptre is missing. Furthermore...

..Bordurian shops were looted again yesterday. These incidents are of course the work of agitators in the pay of a foreign power, but we are faced with a dangerous situation. And if Your Majesty appears before the crowds without the sceptre, I fear...

Rest assured, Prime Minister, there will be no bloodshed. I will abdica te.

No, Sir, you will not abdicate...

! TINTIN! ?

Your Majesty, I have your sceptre with me now!

Saved!

Here it is!... I... Great snakes! I've lost it on the way!

Lucky I saw the sceptre fall out of his pocket!

!

???

Saved!... I am saved!... How happy this makes me!

Saved for the moment only, Sir. I have discovered something else...

I found these on the ruffians I went after.

'Seizure of power'!... And it's signed Müsstler! ...Müsstler, the leader of the Iron Guard!

Not a moment to lose! Arrest Müsstler and his associates at once!

Yes, Sire!...

General, the review of the army will not take place tomorrow as arranged. By 8 a.m., crack regiments will occupy defensive positions along the frontier. And take over all the strategic points which the rebels plan to attack...

Very good, Sire!

Some hours later...

COCKADOODLEDOO

BOOM

BOOM

Guns!...

Come in!

Oh, it's you!...What is all that firing for?

That?...

They are firing a salute for St. Vladimir's Day... Hurry up and dress, or we shall miss the procession.

And so the royal carriage leaves the palace... the King, smiling, bare-headed, is holding the Sceptre of Ottokar in his hand... A great roar of welcome greets His Majesty, a roar which fades only when the strains of our national anthem swell from a thousand voices ...

And now the King is once more in his palace. Time and again the delirious crowds have called His Majesty back on to the balcony to receive their tumultuous acclaim. But now he is seated here in the Throne Room, where an investiture is taking place ...

My Lords, Ladies and Gentlemen. Never in our long history has the Order of the Golden Pelican been conferred upon a foreigner. But today with the full agreement of Our ministers, We bestow this high distinction upon Mr. Tintin, to express Our gratitude for the great services he has rendered to Our country..

Tintin, Knight of the Order of the Golden Pelican...

Hurrah!... Hurrah!...

Some days later...

MINISTRY OF THE INTERIOR

OFFICE OF THE MINISTER

I expect you will like to hear the result of our enquiries. You already know that Müsstler, leader of the Iron Guard, has been arrested with most of his followers. Calling themselves the Iron Guard they were in fact the Z.Z.R.K., the Zyldav Zentral Revolutzionär Komitzät, whose aims were the deposition of our King, and the annexation of our country by Borduria...

Professor Alembick was also arrested at Müsstler's home where he hid after the theft of the sceptre. This little book was found on him...

Slassanov, Igor. Ambassador. A very close friend. Met him in Belgrade in 1913 at a sigillographical congress. Gave me a letter of introduction to study national archives in Klow. He

Kavaromitch Syldavian Secret Agent. Keeps an eye on Syldavian organisations abroad. Pretends to be an artist. Suspect... to suspect... before of him!

LIQUIDATED!

I know him. He's the man who collapsed in my room! But look!... That's me!...

Tintin. Reporter. Brought back my briefcase. Showed him my collection of seals. Mentioned my visit to Zyld... Said I needed a secretary. Promised to send him my book on

DON'T TRUST HIM!

It's incredible!... But what was this note book for?...

So that they would know everyone who went to see the real Professor Alembick... Here is another photograph found at Müsstler's house which is the key to the puzzle...

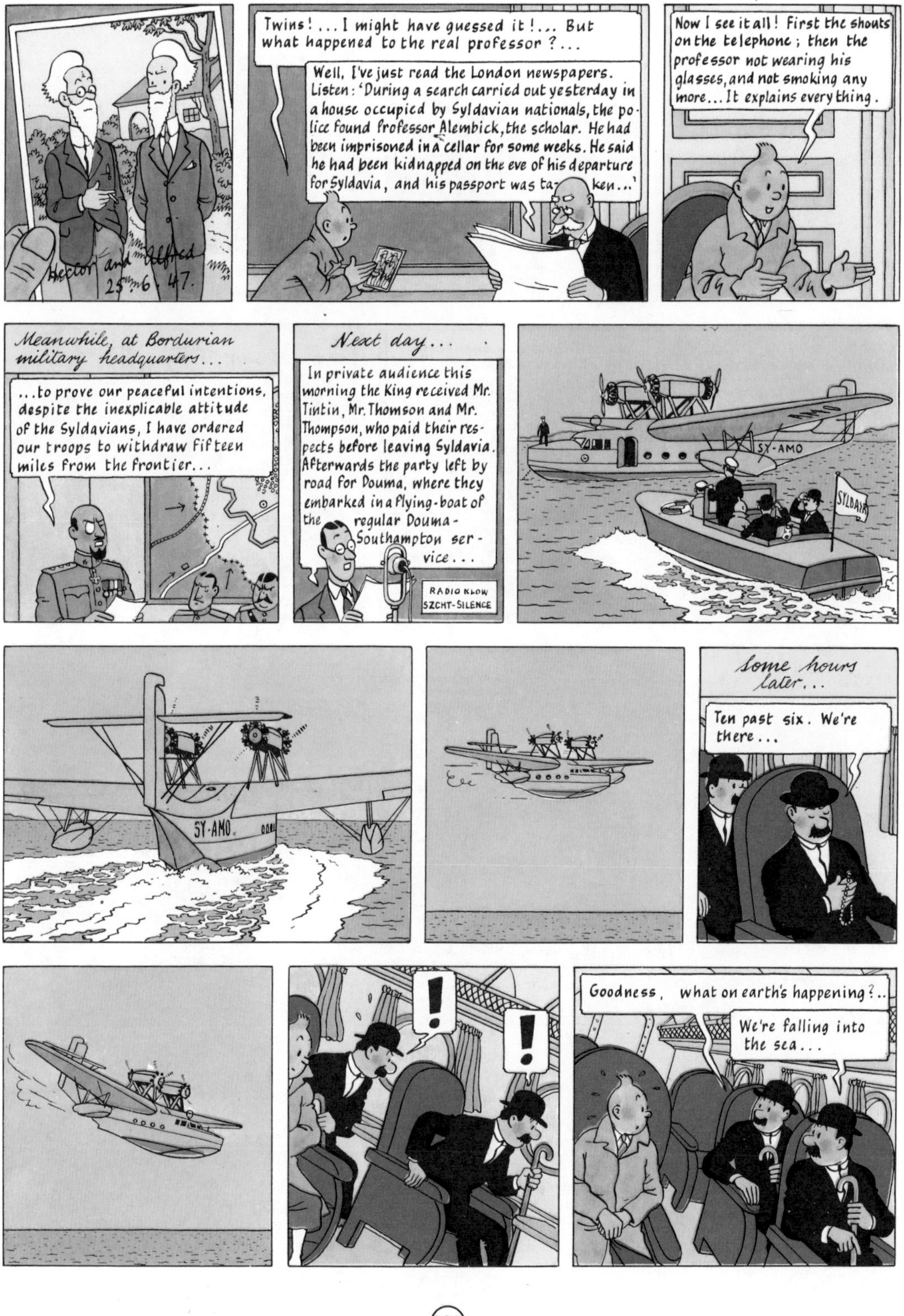
Hector and Alfred 25·6·47.
Twins! ... I might have guessed it! ... But what happened to the real professor? ...
Well, I've just read the London newspapers. Listen: 'During a search carried out yesterday in a house occupied by Syldavian nationals, the police found professor Alembick, the scholar. He had been imprisoned in a cellar for some weeks. He said he had been kidnapped on the eve of his departure for Syldavia, and his passport was taken...'
Now I see it all! First the shouts on the telephone; then the professor not wearing his glasses, and not smoking any more... It explains everything.
Meanwhile, at Bordurian military headquarters...
...to prove our peaceful intentions, despite the inexplicable attitude of the Syldavians, I have ordered our troops to withdraw fifteen miles from the frontier...
Next day...
In private audience this morning the King received Mr. Tintin, Mr. Thomson and Mr. Thompson, who paid their respects before leaving Syldavia. Afterwards the party left by road for Douma, where they embarked in a flying-boat of the regular Douma-Southampton service...
RADIO KLOW
SZCHT-SILENCE
SY-AMO
SY-AMO
Some hours later...
Ten past six. We're there...
!
!
Goodness, what on earth's happening?..
We're falling into the sea...

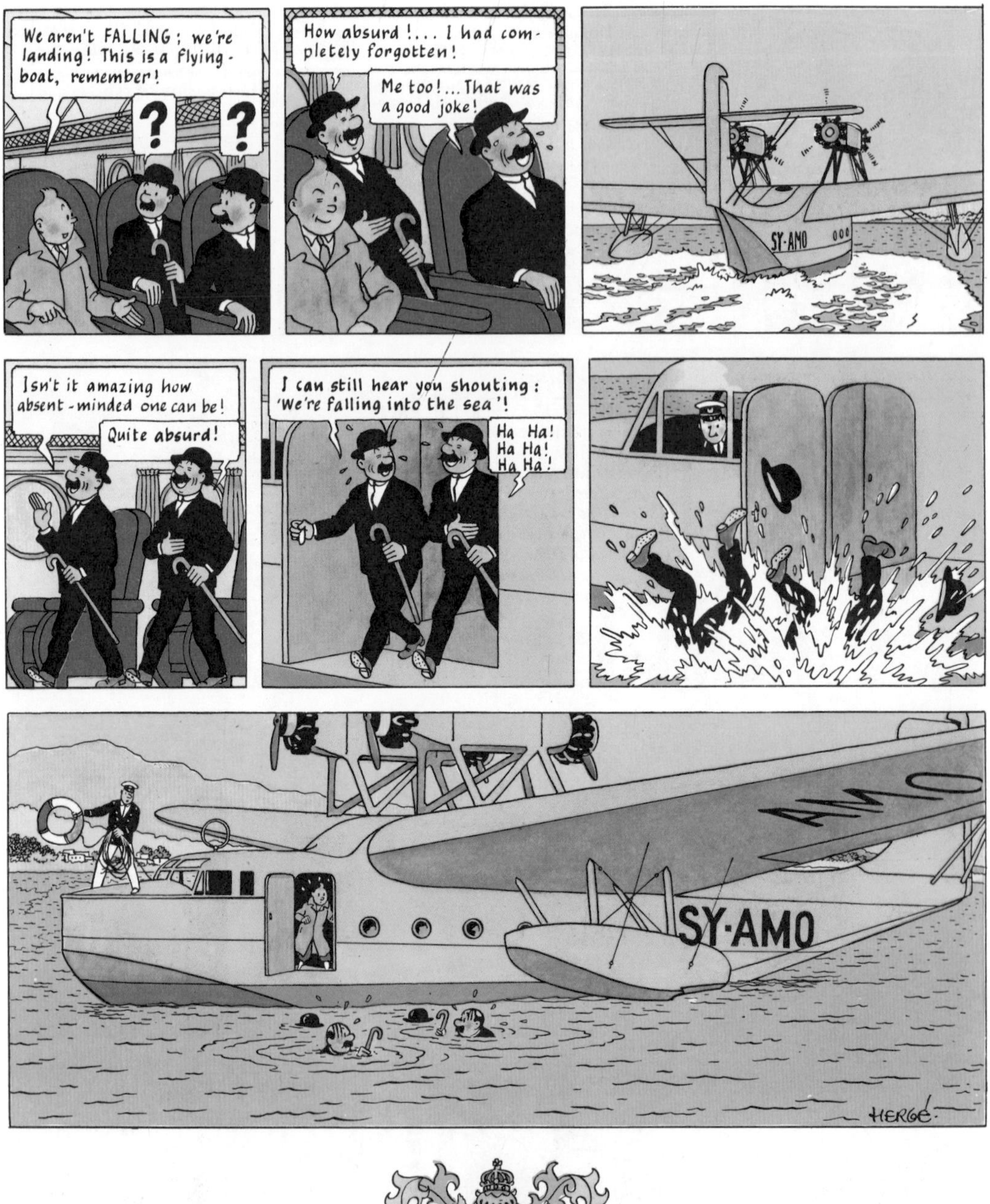
We aren't FALLING ; we're landing! This is a flying-boat, remember!
?
?
How absurd!... I had completely forgotten!
Me too!... That was a good joke!
SY-AMO
Isn't it amazing how absent-minded one can be!
Quite absurd!
I can still hear you shouting: 'We're falling into the sea'!
Ha Ha! Ha Ha! Ha Ha!
AMO
SY-AMO
HERGÉ

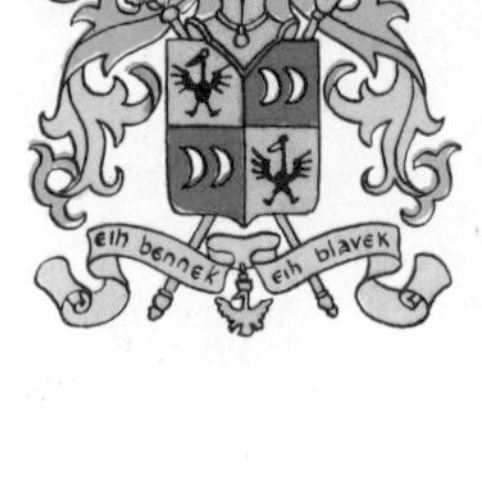
eih bennek eih blavek

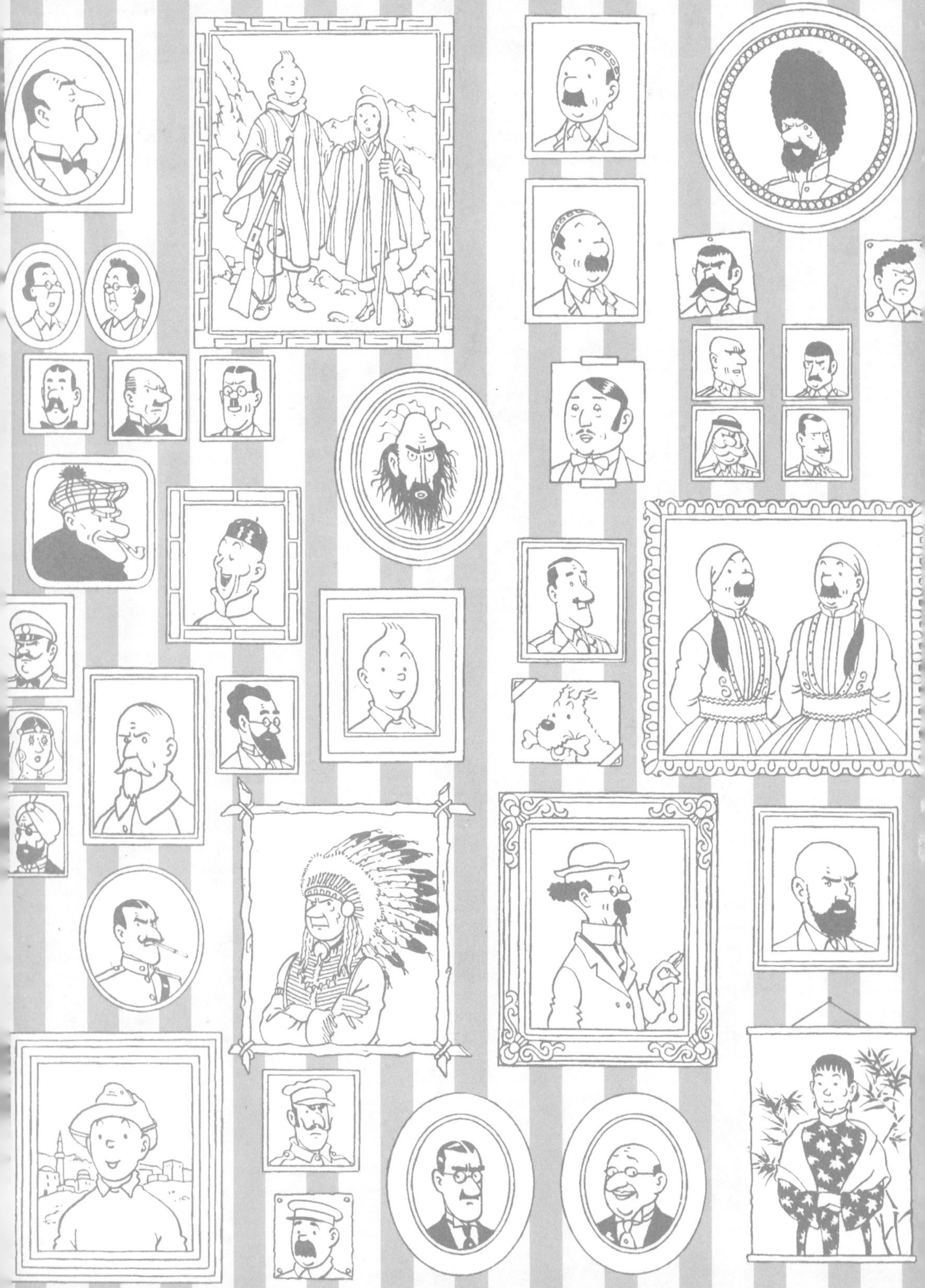